SUPER PENGUIN

Rob Witzel

DORRANCE
PUBLISHING CO
EST. 1920
PITTSBURGH, PENNSYLVANIA 15238

Dorrance Publishing Co
585 Alpha Drive
Pittsburgh, PA 15238
Visit our website at *www.dorrancebookstore.com*

ISBN: 978-1-6376-4145-3
eISBN: 978-1-6376-4783-7

For Parker

Special Thanks to Halley, Mom, Dad, Gardner
& Cindy for all your help along the way!

Dear Reader,

Welcome to Earth. Well it's technically Earth....just not the Earth you know....

Ok, so imagine when God began His creation that He simultaneously created different versions of the same existence. There's your version where everything exists the way you see it today. There's another version where fire never exists (not a lot of fun), and another version without gravity (loads of fun). Other versions started the same as your Earth but with tweaks down the line, like "What if the Great Flood never happened?" or "What if mayonnaise was never invented? (That one had a much bigger chain reaction than you'd think!) All these versions exist at the same time playing out in their own way. Some versions change rapidly while others have gone millennia without much of a difference at all.

Well, there's also a version where humans never existed. That's the version of Earth where this story takes place. Believe it or not, it's eerily similar to your version of Earth.

Without a dominant species, animals became much more advanced and started doing all the same things humans did. They physically evolved too: standing upright and with improved motor functions. Well, except for fish...those things are just dumb and never evolved.

After a few hundred years, the animals learned how to speak a universal language (we translated this to English for your reading pleasure). Time passed, and as they began to talk to each other, the food chain shattered, and the predator/prey relationship disappeared (except for fish, now one of the seven food groups!) By the year 1620, this version of Earth was just as advanced as your version is in the 2020s. Animals wore clothes, drove cars, and created all the technology you have today before your "human Earth" even had electricity.

In this story, you'll witness the beginning of a new era on *No Human Earth*. The beginning of superheroes. Ordinary citizens who become extraordinary and use it for the betterment of those around them. And of course with superheroes...come super villains...

I hope you enjoy their story,
Rob

Paul Frost, a penguin, sat across from his friend and colleague Annie Freese, a polar bear. They were seated at their favorite table, in their favorite restaurant, a diner called "Tina's." It wasn't a very big restaurant. The entrance was in the northeast corner. As soon as you walked in there were five four-seater booths next to windows, across the aisle from the booths was bar seating that faced the kitchen.

Paul and Annie preferred to sit in the middle booth for no particular reason beyond that's where they normally sat until it became tradition to sit there.

"First night covering the pros. Are you excited?" Annie asked as she bit into her anchovy club sandwich.

"I don't know if excited is the right word," the penguin replied as he stirred his otherwise untouched coffee nervously. "What's a word for nervous, anxious, and a little bit terrified all at once?"

"Eh," Annie responded as she took in another mouthful of sandwich. When she swallowed the bite, she wiped her mouth with her paw. "I'd still say 'excited'.... sounds better." She took a drink of her water. "Besides, what are you nervous about? You've done tons of articles on college and high school games, and you love hockey. You know more about that sport than anyone I know."

"Oh, I'm not nervous about the game," Paul answered, still stirring his coffee and yet to take a drink. "It's this meeting I just had with Trunk. He keeps telling everyone their stories aren't 'exciting enough' right before they get canned. So, he *reminded* me how important it is for my article to be exciting no matter how dull the game is."

"Then do it," Annie stated simply as she scarfed down the last bite of her sandwich. "You always overthink these things. Get out of your head. You're a good writer. You got the beat because you earned it, and not because of anything else. If the game's boring, then make it exciting, and if it's really boring then talk about all the allegations about the Egrets losing on purpose."

"Yeah, that has been pretty crazy. All the fan pages and conspiracy theorists are going nuts. Do you think it's true? Any tips from the crime division?"

"Well….and this is off the record, ok?"

Paul gave an affirming nod.

Annie leaned in, and, in a hushed tone, continued, "There's definitely something going on. No players have been linked to it, but there's been some tips coming into the police department about illegal gambling and point shaving. It's being investigated heavily, but nothing found yet."

"Yikes! That's pretty intense." Paul chugged his now cold coffee and then pulled out his phone and checked the time. "Alright, well I better get going."

***

Wally Whax, a turtle, sat down in front of the microphone for the post-game press conference. The star of the reigning league champion Eagle City Egrets began with his opening remarks. "I don't really know what to say," Wally said seemingly unbothered by the loss. "We came in as the favorites, and we lost again. That's it, plain and simple. We're trying really hard, but the pucks not going into the net. I'll take any questions now…"

Hooves, wings and arms shot up.

"Alright...um you. The deer in the second row"

"Hey Wally, Janet Doe from NSN in Buckington. Last year, at this point in the season you were leading the Egrets with 20 goals and a 7-0 record. Now, you're sitting at 1-6 with just two goals. What's different this year?"

"Well, like I said, we are doing our best, but so is everyone else out there. Defenses around the league have stepped up. We're going to keep getting better and go from there."

The oldest reporter in the room, an alligator, raised his arm.

"What's up, Mr. LaGarto?"

"Can you elaborate on what's better about the opponents' defense?"

"I would say they are just really prepared. A lot of the plays that had worked in the past, these guys are ready for. They are doing their homework and know a lot of our plays. They seem to be adjusting to our new ones too. Alright, one more question. The penguin in the back."

The newest reporter in the conference room, Paul Frost stood to ask his question. "Hi Wally....um... I'm Paul Frost with the *Inquirer*." He paused to reconsider what he was about to ask, but asked it anyway. "There've been some allegations—"

"I'm gonna stop you right there." The turtle's mood suddenly souring. "Is this about those allegations about me throwing games?"

"Well... yeah," Paul responded. "It just seems—"

Wally cut him off again, "You really think I'm losing on purpose or point shaving or whatever you eggheads call it? Guys like you are pathetic, man. You've got no talent besides telling other people about my talent! I carry this team to championship after championship, and the moment we get off to a slow start, you think we're doing it on purpose? And for what! I'm the highest paid player in the league! You think I need a little extra spending money? I make more in one game than you will all year. Get your fifteen minutes of fame some-where else punk!"

Wally turned to his agent, also a turtle, as he stood. "I don't want that egghead at another game. Take care of that," and he left the room.

Every eye in the room was on Paul, each with their own look of disgust. The rookie reporter avoided the glares, packed his things into his backpack, and went to write his story.

***

Paul walked into the newsroom. The room was split into four sections each with four desks clumped together. Down the middle aisle was a long row of carpet that led straight to the editor's room. The sports-desk clump was immediately to the left upon entering the room. Paul headed for his desk, which sat facing away from Trunk's office. The penguin sat in his chair and placed his backpack on the floor. Paul quietly trans-ferred its contents to his desk and while reaching into his bag, caught the eye of his boss and editor, Tom Trunk. Trunk was an elephant, and, while all elephants are large, he was particu-larly large for his kind. His reputation for a short fuse and low tolerance for mistakes made for rocky relationships with even his best writers and staff. Trunk was staring at, and through, Paul.

"What the heck, Frost!" boomed the elephant.

Paul froze. He whispered to himself, "Maybe he's talking about something else. Deep breath. He probably doesn't know."

"Your first day on the beat, and you're already accusing the BEST PLAYER IN LEAGUE OF CHEATING! What the heck were you thinking?"

Still whispering to himself, "Okay, he definitely knows. Stay calm…"

"I'm talking to you, Frost!" the elephant roared now right behind him.

"Well, sir...um...you said to make the story exciting.... and there's been rumors and.... I just thought ..."

"RUMORS?" The elephant's voice grew louder, and every eye in the room was now watching the confrontation. "You're gonna report on rumors from some two-bit fan page?" He paused to catch his breath and noticed the attention on them. "Change of venue. MY OFFICE! NOW!" Trunk pointed toward his door, and the penguin followed orders. Paul sat in one of the two chairs opposite the desk.

"I didn't say you could sit!" Trunk boomed.

Paul shot back to his feet.

"Take a seat," the elephant ordered before he turned on the television. On the screen was an image of Paul at the hockey press conference. The subject of his own sports segment, Paul's implied allegations were going viral. Tom, slightly more collected than he had been at the start of the conversation, sat down at his desk. "Paul, your job is to report on the sports news, not to create it or be part of it."

"I get that, but—"

"No buts." Tom's temper was starting back up. "Just write about the game." And with that, Tom motioned for Paul to leave the room.

Paul walked back to his desk. The fact that he was even writing a story was probably a good sign that he was keeping his job...at least until the story was turned in. When Paul got back to his desk clump, he was met by a young, cocky, up-and-coming mallard by the name of Howie.

"Good start, Pete. First day on the new gig and you drag the paper through the mud. I knew he should have given me the beat!"

"Paul," the penguin corrected.

"What?"

"My name is Paul"

"Ha! Does it matter? Didn't Trunk just fire you?"

"No...well, not yet I guess. He sent me back here to write."

"So, are you going to write about the game, or...?"

"Or what?"

"Or are you going to report about the juicy, exciting scandal?"

"Nice try, Howie. I'd have to be pretty stupid to do that and think I'd keep my job."

"Ha ha! You're right...QUACK!"

"What the heck was that?"

"Sorry. Sometimes, when I get excited, QUACK! I quack, uncontrolla—QUACK! uncontrollably, and I can't QUACK stop!" The mallard ran out of the room and toward the breakroom.

Paul wrote his story, emailed it to the editor, and went home.

***

BZZZZZZZZT BZZZZZZZZT BZZZZZZZZZT

Paul woke to his cell phone vibrating. He rolled over toward his nightstand, grabbed his phone, and saw alerts for twelve missed calls with several voicemails. The penguin tapped his phone and saw they were all from his friend Annie.

Paul listened to the first voicemail.

"Hey Paul. Its Annie. You'd uh... better get down to the office quick. Trunk's not too excited about your story in today's paper and—" Her words were interrupted by the sound of flying furniture crashing into a wall. "Uh, yeah just get here, ok?"

Confused, Paul went to collect his copy of the newspaper outside his door. He unwound the rubber band and shuffled to the sports section. In the premiere placement, Paul saw the headline "Egrets Caught Cheating, Refuse to Admit It." Paul's eyes drifted to the by-line...PAUL FROST!

He had been set up! A rage overcame Paul. His whole

body became tense, and he let out an aggravated "Howie!"

He didn't know how, and he had no way to prove it, but the penguin knew this was the doing of his new workplace rival Howie.

The phone started buzzing again. Annie. This time, he answered. "Yeah, I saw it. I'm getting ready now and am on my way." Annie didn't answer at first, and instead Paul heard more furniture crashing into objects.

"Okay," she eventually let out.

Paul skipped a shower, brushed his beak, changed into his work clothes, and headed toward the chaos.

***

The newsroom looked like a warzone.

Desks flipped over; others smashed in half. Papers, pens, and desk debris were scattered all over the floor. Paul scanned the destruction. He noticed a chair thrown so hard into the wall that it became stuck. "I wonder whose chair that is?" he whispered to himself. The penguin looked to his desk: chairless. "I thought that chair looked familiar," he monologued as he glanced back at it. Paul was so caught up in the destruction that he missed the one-elephant stampede headed his direction. Steps before an assault, Annie stepped between her boss and her best friend.

The rampaging editor abruptly halted. For many reasons, he didn't mess with Annie. Most notably, she would obviously beat him in a scuffle. Paul knew Annie likely just saved him a trip to the emergency room.

Disgruntled and discombobulated, Trunk screamed, "MY OFFICE NOW, FROST!" as he pointed.

Paul shot Annie a look that said "Thanks" with a dash of "Nice knowing ya," then he followed the elephant's orders as the rest of the newsroom gazed. As the penguin walked, he saw Howie in the crowd. Paul didn't look at him long, but as he looked away, he heard "QUACK!" Paul didn't know how, but Howie's excitement removed any doubt as to who was behind this setup.

Trunk turned his attention to the audience. "Get back to work!" The elephant took a look around the aftermath of the office "...and someone clean this place up for cryin' out loud!" The crowd scurried to the closest chore.

Paul walked over the threshold. Unlike the night before, he wasn't alone with Trunk. Sitting in Trunk's leather desk chair was Trunk's father and owner of the newspaper, Donald Trunk. The senior Trunk dressed much more professionally than his son. His navy blue suit perfectly creased, his blood red tie shined, and his hair was so perfectly coiffed that it almost looked fake. Standing to Mr. Trunk's right was his lawyer, a weasel. The lawyer stood so still, Paul wasn't sure if he was fake too.

Paul sat in the vacant chair opposite Mr. Trunk.

"Thomas, why don't you go back out there and help clean up your mess." The son, usually argumentative, knew this was not a time to challenge his father. He left the room and closed the door behind him. Donald's attention went directly to the penguin. "Mr. Frost, I presume you know why you're here right now, so I'll just cut to the chase. First off, what you did was reckless and put us in a very vulnerable situation."

"But Mr. Trunk..."

Before Paul could continue, the elephant shot him a disapproving stare, stopping the penguin in his tracks. Mr. Trunk took a moment to collect his thoughts and continued.

"I've spoken with my lawyer Mr. Zuckerkorn." The weasel nodded, proving once and for all that he wasn't a statue. Paul still wasn't sure about the elephant's hair/wig. "Now that your story has been unwantedly published, you've created two possible scenarios that may play out. Our paper wants to be prepared for both. So...."

"Scenario 1. What you said was false. We will likely hear

from Mr. Whax's lawyers, and he will want to sue for defamation of his character and libel. You'll be fired, and with the information we've gathered, we have enough to prove our newspaper had plausible deniability, so you exclusively will be at fault."

Paul had a lump in his throat. He cleared it and said, "So, um.... what's the other scenario? I don't want to jump to conclusions, but it has to be better, right?" Paul then silently thought to himself, "Please be better. Please be better...." Until Mr. Trunk started speaking again.

"Scenario 2 is better, but we aren't sure how likely it is that it will happen." He paused and took a drink from his coffee mug. "Scenario 2 is the only reason we haven't fired you already. That's because Scenario Number 2 is that you were right. Even though what you've done is certainly grounds for termination, if you cracked this case open, we want you working for us. Not to mention the hit to our credibility if we fired you for simply exposing the truth."

The elephant took another sip, slightly longer than the first one.

"*So* here is our immediate plan. As of today, you are suspended indefinitely until we can figure out which scenario plays out. In the meantime, we want you as far away from the situation as possible. Because of your actions there are league officials and even members of the police force looking into your accusations. If we see or hear that you're meddling in their investigation, we will terminate you for insubordination. Do I make myself perfectly clear?"

Paul nodded.

"Good. Then please see yourself out. We will have Miss Freese collect your things when we remove them from the drywall."

***

"Okay, so what the heck happened?" Annie asked as she took a bite from her anchovy club. The two sat in their booth at Tina's, recapping the day

"I really don't know for sure." Paul took a French fry from his plate, dragged it through a dollop of ketchup, and then tossed it into his beak. "But I know Howie is behind it. He basically told me he wanted my beat, and then a story I didn't write shows up...."

"So, what are you gonna do?" Annie asked and then bit into her sandwich again.

"I have no idea. What do you think I should do?"

Annie, still with a mouthful of sandwich, responded, "Yoo godda proo dat Whax is a chee-uh."

Paul glared at his friend. "You are one disgusting bear."

Annie finished chewing her mouthful, swallowed, and then tried again. "You gotta prove that Whax is a cheater." She took another bite of the club sandwich, chewed completely, and continued. "We don't know specifics, but there's definitely something going on. Maybe it's Whax or maybe it's someone else...*or someone's...*"

"Okay, so what do you propose we do?" Paul asked.

"Well, you need to sneak around the hockey arena and look for some clues."

"Me? I just got banned publicly by Whax and told by Trunk's dad to stay away or I'm fired. Why don't you do it?"

Annie laughed. "You ever see a bear sneak in some place? I'm like ten times your size. They'll see me coming from a mile away."

"That still doesn't explain why it has to be me. Didn't you say the police were looking into it?"

"It's not a dangerous stakeout or something. You're just looking around for clues. You still have your credentials, right? Those are good for the season, and you have access to locker rooms before and after the game. You can practically waltz right in!"

"I guess you're right," Paul said reluctantly accepting his assignment.

"Of course, I'm right," Annie said as she tossed the last bite of sandwich into her mouth. Then she jokingly added, "Just don't wear that hideous hat of yours."

Paul's facial expression suddenly turned solemn. He reached into his backpack and pulled out an ugly, brown bowler. "This one?" he asked as he set the hat on the table.

"Yes! That thing is awful; where did you find it?"

Choked up with emotion, Paul responded, "It was my dad's..." He paused to collect himself. "He was at my house the night before the fire, and he left it...and... it's the only thing of his that I have..." The penguin wiped a tear away.

"Oh my gosh, Paul. I'm so sorry, I didn't know..."

Paul sniffled one last time, his eyes red. "It's okay, Annie." He looked the hat over. "It is pretty ugly." The two friends chuckled together. Then Paul said, "Well I better get going. I'll talk to you later tonight."

***

Paul pulled into the parking lot fifteen minutes before the game. Tonight's matchup was the Eagle City Egrets versus the Rockville Rockets. The penguin wore his usual uniform: a short-sleeved, buttoned-up shirt, one with pockets to hold his pens. He wore his dad's bowler too. The penguin hoped it would help disguise his look, and maybe provide him a little luck. Paul threw his press pass lanyard around his neck, grabbed his normal supplies (so it looked like he was working), and made his way for the door.

As he walked, his pocket buzzed—a text message from Annie, "Hey, Trunk has Howie working the game tonight. Make sure he doesn't see you, He'd do anything to get your job for good."

"Thanks," Paul messaged back as he made his way into the stadium. The suspended reporter walked the normal reporter path and into the doors labeled "PRESS ONLY." A middle-aged hippopotamus that always watched the door was in her usual spot. "Excuse me, sir," she interjected. Paul lifted the bowler, and before he could say a word, Paul heard the hippo's voice turn sour. "Oh....it's you...I didn't recognize you with that hat.... go on in." She ended with a disgusted *huff* and a hateful glare. Paul had never exchanged names with the guard, but then he quickly remembered the media buzz around him. Once Paul was out of the hippo's sight, he changed course, away from the press box seats and into the regular attendee seats.

The arena was sparse. With the losing streak, this certainly wasn't a surprise, but it would definitely impact Paul's ability to blend in with the crowd. The penguin found a seat nearest the visitors' locker rooms, and he waited for an opportunity to investigate their area. Paul knew the team's routine. After each of the three periods, they would return to the locker room, but after the third period, they would shake hands on the ice followed by a trip to the media room for post-game interviews. Paul knew he'd have the most time to look if he got into the locker room just as the third period started. He'd check the visitors' room first as the security detail there was typically lighter.

The hockey match was turning into another abysmal performance by the Egrets. Based on recent history, the home team should have scored easily and often, an "easy win "; however, the game was once again an ironic one that had the Egrets losing 1-0. The team's star Whax had taken at least twenty shots, and every one of them was stopped by the goalie, a frog, Billy Ribbetts. Ribbetts was a good, but not great, goalie—nowhere near as good as Whax. But tonight Ribbetts was having the best game of his career, shutting down the Egrets and their star.

The first two periods seemed to drag on forever to Paul as he nervously yet eagerly waited for his opportunity. Finally, the third period was about to begin. Paul rose from his seat and went toward the locker room. There was a maze of white brick hallways that would cause anyone who didn't know their way to be lost for weeks. The penguin had only been here once before but tried to walk with confidence. If he was seen by a security guard, Paul wanted to give the impression that he knew what he was doing and where he was going. Paul saw a sign in the shape of an arrow:

VISITORS' LOCKER ROOM

The penguin peered around the corner. The players were leaving the room and heading away from him. When the last player left, Paul retreated back around the corner. He stood up straight, dusted himself off, and walked toward the locker room.

At the door, Paul was met by a large dalmatian, nearly twice Paul's height and weight. The guard wore an earpiece in his left ear and a bright yellow shirt with "SECURITY" in big, bold, black letters. The guard dog's shirt was filled with bulging muscles; it looked like the shirt could explode from trying to contain them at any moment. It was obvious Paul wasn't forcing his way in and was going to have to talk his way past the guard.

"Um...excuse me, sir," Paul said while fumbling with his backpack. "I think I left my notebook in there when I was doing an interview between periods. I know exactly where I left it. Can you let me in really quick?" Paul took off his credential and handed it to the guard.

The dog looked over the badge, flipped it, and handed it back to Paul. He took out a key ring with hundreds of gold and sliver keys. The dog shuffled through the collection and then unlocked the door. "You've got thirty seconds. Make it quick," he said as he opened the door. Paul walked inside, and the door swung closed behind him. Paul slowly and silently dead-bolted the door, then he grabbed a nearby chair and wedged it under the handle to buy just a little bit more time if necessary. Paul started at the closest locker. He delicately shuffled through the locker. Nothing. With just one locker investigated, Paul heard the front door handle jiggle. The guard had just discovered that Paul had locked the door.

The penguin moved to the next locker, and his strategy changed. Paul frantically pawed through it. Nothing.

The sound of the clanging deadbolt was now the sound of the door ramming into the wedged chair.

"Hey! Get out here now!" the dog's voice boomed. Paul continued moving as a fast as he could.

The third locker was twice as big. The captain's received a double-wide locker as a reward. It was Ribbetts's locker. Paul scrambled through a laundry pile and, underneath, found two playbooks. The first belonged to the Rockets; the second was an Egrets playbook. Paul rummaged through it quickly and saw the name of a different Egret player, Michael Myles, a cheetah who rarely played in the games.

Before Paul could investigate the playbook anymore, the chair holding the door began to give way. Next to the hinge side of the door was an extra-large laundry bin. Paul left the book with the mess he made, leapt inside, and covered himself with the dirty clothes. Moments later the door was smashed open. The door smacked the laundry bin hard, but the dog angrily stepped into the room, never glancing in Paul's direction. The guard scanned the room quickly. With no immediate sign of Paul, the dog continued into the back of the locker room and went around a corner.

Paul, seizing his opportunity, leapt out of the bin and exited the room. The penguin headed directly to the exit and then to his car. Once he got there, Paul frantically hopped inside and called Annie.

"Annie, it's me. Are you alone?" he said in a panicked, out of breath voice.

"Yes. Are you okay? What's going on?"

"I just left the stadium. It's not Whax, but there is definitely something fishy going on. Whax isn't losing on purpose. His opponents just know what's coming. I found Michael Myles's copy of the playbook in the goalie's locker. If he's been doing this all season long...."

"Then it has to be someone local who's paying him," Annie finished his sentence. "Paul, you've got to trail Myles. Whoever he's working for could meet him tonight to pay him. There's no way they'll do that in the stadium with witnesses."

The exit doors opened, and a crowd of subdued fans began to trickle out. The game was over. "I gotta go. Game just finished, so I got about fifteen minutes until Myles leaves. I'll call you when I know more."

Paul ended the call and waited.

Minutes later Paul saw Myles but almost didn't recognize him. The cheetah had a long brown trench coat and a matching bowler hat with sunglasses on despite it being night. The star players usually wore a similar outfit as to avoid the fans, but guys like Myles often wanted the attention and the fame. Myles began to walk away from the players' parking lot. If the cheetah wasn't meeting his secret employer, he was certainly dressed like he was doing something wrong...

Paul got out of his car and walked double time to catch up with Myles while keeping just enough distance between them to see Myles without being detected. The cheetah walked under a light post, pulled out his phone, and appeared to make a call. "I'm here." Paul could barely make out the cheetah's words, and moments later a white van stopped in front of Myles with DRAGONCORP printed on the side.

Suddenly, from behind Paul, a voice yelled, "THERE HE IS!" The penguin turned and saw the dalmatian with a team of four more guard dogs.

Paul ran away in a path perpendicular to both the guards and the van.

He turned down an alley and kept running.

Dead End.

No ladder to climb.

No gate to hurdle over.

No doors to walk through.

The penguin could hear the guards' footsteps headed his way.

Suddenly, a door appeared directly behind Paul.

It opened, and a large, clawed paw extended out.

The mysterious hand grabbed Paul by the collar, pulling him inside.

The door closed and then vanished from sight.

***

A large, muscular Komodo dragon stood behind his large, wooden desk in his large, elegant office. The reptile wore only the finest, most expensive suits, custom made for his tail to fit through the back. His midnight black suit jacket matched his pants and was half a shade darker than the dress shirt he wore underneath. Everything else in the room, from the desk to the picture frames, matched his elegance. He waited for his next appointment.

KNOCK, KNOCK

"Come in," he beckoned.

A hyena let himself in equipped with a clipboard and pen. "Good evening, General. I have the results from the game you asked for."

"Oh yes, tell me how we did?"

"Well, sir, there's some good news and some bad news."

The hyena nervously swallowed before he went on. "The good news is the Egrets lost again, and there's still no sign of detection. In fact, most of the attention is on that turtle instead of our guy. The bad news is that with all that attention, we aren't sure how much longer we can do this without being found out. Mr. Myles thought he may have been followed when delivering the team's next game plan. We have it, so the next game won't be affected, but again I'm not sure how long we can..."

"I understand. Place bets for tomorrow's game. Double the usual bet, and then we'll be done."

"Will do, General," the hyena said as he jotted down notes. "Also, there's someone here to meet with you. Said his name was Dr. Pigg—"

"Ah yes," the reptile interrupted. "Send him in right away."

The hyena left, and moments later the door opened without a knock. A short, giddy pig entered the room with a bow tie around his neck and a skip in his step.

"General Talon, it's a pleasure to meet you, sir," the swine spoke as he extended his hoof for a shake. "I'm quite excited to be here, sir."

Talon accepted the handshake. "The pleasure is all mine, Doctor. Your resume looked quite impressive, and we certainly could use a man of your...talents...on staff. I do have one concern though."

As Talon paused, three armed hyenas entered the room. The last one deadbolted the door shut. Talon stood.

"Here at DragonCorp, we do what needs to be done." Talon walked around to the front of his desk and sat on its edge, uncomfortably close to Pigg. "Sometimes, we bend the rules, and sometimes, we downright break them." He smiled maniacally.

Pigg's expression of excitement transformed into an uneasy stare. "So...um... the rumors of you being tied to the criminal underground.... they're true?"

"Doctor, Doctor, Doctor," Talon said with a smile. "Do I look like the kind of reptile who would sell dangerous weapons to a bunch of petty crooks?"

Dr. Pigg could have been mistaken for a statue he was so still and silent.

"Of course not. Those crooks all work for me. Robbing banks, rigging sports bets—all just part of our fundraising efforts," he said matter-of-factly.

"Wh-what do you want me for?" the doctor asked.

The general rose to his feet and stood behind the pig's chair. "Well, you see doctor...I have quite a bit of power, and even more money, but..."

Talon spun the swine's chair around to face him. His head darted towards the doctor's. Eyes wide open, the lizard's razor-sharp teeth showing, he exclaimed, "I WANT MORE!"

His face stayed close to his guest's, the volume of his voice lowered, but the intensity remained.

"With my plan, we will first take over the city then eventually the world—piece by piece, place by place, until I have it all!"

Talon straightened, adjusted his suit jacket, and walked back to his desk chair. As he sat, he continued, "And for that to happen, we need a man of your talents."

"And.... what if... I...decline your offer?" Dr. Pigg trembled.

"Now, of course, Dr. Pigg, I am a very reasonable reptile, and taking this position on our team is your choice. I only want employees working for me who *want* to work for me." Talon paused and leaned back in his chair. "However, I just shared quite a bit of confidential information about our corporation, so I can't just let you leave and pretend like nothing happened."

General Talon leaned back in his chair, brought his hands to his chest, and interlocked his claws.

"The way I see it, you have two options. Option 1, *which I highly recommend*, is you accept my offer and begin working first thing tomorrow morning. One of my men will fetch your things from your home. You'll have your own quarters here and work on this project for me. We'll provide everything you could possibly need while you're here all expenses paid." Talon smiled again. "And when you're done, you'll be paid a ridiculous amount of money and be the world's wealthiest hog."

The smile disappeared. Talon's voice lost its friendly demeanor, and he continued, "Option 2 is those three hyenas behind you tie you up and throw you into the incinerator with the last guy who told me no."

***

Paul was quickly pulled through the hidden door.

Startled and confused, the penguin turned around and was faced with a large but damaged lion. The jungle cat was not much older than Paul but was in severely worse health. The lion wore a Hawaiian patterned shirt, an eye patch over his left eye, and walked with a cane. He hunched over slightly, and his long, stringy mane hung over much of his face.

"Shhhh," the lion whispered with one finger over his mouth.

The two stood silently as they listened intently; the watch dogs were just outside the door.

"Where'd he go?" one asked with no answer. The sounds of crashing trashcans and hands rustling through garbage echoed through the brick walls.

"C'mon, he must be around here somewhere," and the dogs left the alleyway.

Inside, the lion peered through the peephole and then spoke at his normal volume. "Looks like they're gone," he said as he walked toward a large, reclining chair.

Confused, Paul remained silent as he gazed around the room. It was plain and cold. No decoration, nothing to entertain guests, only the bare necessities to survive. The space looked to be all one room. To the left of the door was a make-shift kitchen, with a small, waist-high refrigerator that held a microwave on top of it. The stacked appliances stood next to a kitchen table with two wooden chairs. To the right was the beat-up, brown leather reclining chair. A pillow and blanket lied on the floor next to it, insinuating that the chair was also the lion's bed.

"Camouflage door," the lion answered the unasked question. Paul stopped scanning the room, and his attention returned to the lion. "There's a small hologram projector above the door shining down that makes the door look like more of the wall. There's no knob or hinges on the outside either, so it's completely undetectable."

Paul did not respond as he mentally digested his situation.

"Son, you're not being kidnapped and can leave whenever you want. But before you leave, I would like to know why you're investigating DragonCorp. Would you take a seat?" The lion gestured toward one of the kitchen chairs.

"Investigating DragonCorp? I wasn't...I... uh," Paul said as he sat.

"Kid, you aren't in any trouble," the lion interrupted. "But I watched the whole thing from my roof camera." He pointed to a wall that Paul had yet to notice, seven camera monitors and a television. The equipment was obviously installed by amateurs, as no two monitors were the same size and shape. The scenes on the screen were all nearby camera shots. Paul noticed the guard dogs that had pursued him had stopped combing the streets nearby. "You were following one of their associates...oh wait, now I recognize you. You're that penguin who's been all over the news! So, you followed him because... . Okay, I see what happened. You're free to go then, son."

"Wait, so what's going on? If you know something about the point-shaving scandal, I need it! My job depends on it!"

"Kid, there's one reporter that I trust and only one, and my *life* depends on these secrets and certain people not knowing I exist. I assumed you were working with Annie, so that's why I brought you in here. Had I known—"

"Annie? Annie Freese?" Paul interrupted the lion, begging for more information. "I know Annie! Please tell me what's going on!"

"Look, kid, I can't, okay?"

"But..."

"You need to leave now before I make you leave," the lion said as he pointed at the door.

Paul, angry and annoyed, got up and left. He looked down the alleyway for any signs of the watch dogs. Carefully, watching his surroundings, Paul walked back to his car. When he got there, he pulled out his phone and texted Annie.

We need to talk NOW!!!

I know she responded.

"Meet at Tina's?"

"Be there in 10"

***

Paul got to the diner first and sat at their usual table. Minutes later, Annie joined him.

A short, awkward silence was broken with both talking at once Paul's "What's going on?" was simultaneously met with Annie's "Okay, I'll explain."

Annie awkwardly chuckled while Paul remained stoic.

"Okay, so there's a lot you don't know. First off, there are definitely games being rigged, and as far as we know, Whax isn't involved. There are two or three players involved, but that's just scratching the surface."

"Who's 'we'?" Paul questioned, "and scratching the surface of what?"

Annie seemed to struggle with her response as she took a deep breath and leaned closer to Paul. "Right..." She took another deep breath. "Okay..." She took another deep breath, now in a hushed voice.

"Annie, what the heck is going on?" Paul whispered to her.

Another deep breath. "Okay, so this may be a little hard to believe....and don't be mad at me for keeping this a secret.... because you are my best friend and we've known each other forever..."

"Annie!" he exclaimed but still in a hushed voice.

She rambled off in a single breath. "Okay, so the guy you met is named Sampson Hart; he used to be the police chief, but there was an assassination attempt on him. He pretended to be dead, and I was the only one who knew he was alive because of a big cover-up; he thought that DragonCorp was behind it somehow, so I've been helping him investigate it." She let out a sigh at the end.

Astonished, Paul exclaimed, "But why are you—"

"Shhh," Annie quieted him.

Paul whispered again, "But why are you investigating it; if he was the police chief, why can't the police help him?"

"Because he thinks there may be spies within the police department, and if they tried to kill him once, they may try it again. You're now one of just a few people who know he's even alive."

Paul thought for a brief moment. "Okay so how can I help?"

"Well, technically you already have...we didn't know Myles was a part of this, which takes us up to three Egrets helping rig these games. But I'm not really sure what else you can do; like I said, this hockey thing is just scratching the surface. It goes so far beyond that."

"Okay well, if there's anything..."

Annie started thinking out loud. "Come to think of it, we are a very small operation...you already know about Sam...and you're not working so you have tons of free time."

"Easy." Paul chuckled awkwardly. "That emotional wound is still pretty fresh."

"Okay, let me check with him. She pulled out a second phone, one Paul had never seen before. The penguin chuckled, half annoyed, half amused at another secret revealed. Annie typed a message and immediately got a response.

"Okay, you're in." Annie shared. "Be at the safehouse at 5 tomorrow morning. Make sure you aren't followed, keep your gear at home, and bring some coffee, you'll be there awhile."

***

Paul stood at the invisible door equipped with nothing but a coffee and half a dozen donuts. The penguin looked at his watch as 4:59 a.m. rolled into 5:00 exactly. When it did, the door appeared, and the lion was there to hold it open. "Good morning," he said with a smile, oblivious to his idiosyncrasy of waiting until exactly 5 a.m. to let Paul in.

"Good morning," Paul replied as he walked through the doorway. As soon as the door shut, the hologram projector turned back on displaying the camouflage wall once again. He handed the lion the box of donuts. "I brought some breakfast."

"Donuts, huh?" The lion questioned in an annoyed tone. "So, you just assume that because I was a cop that we all love donuts?"

"Well, no, umm... I uh...." Paul awkwardly started.

"I'm just messing with ya, kid." The lion chuckled, and his friendly tone returned. "Besides, it's pretty much true. Ha Ha!" He barehanded a donut and sat in his chair. Between bites, he asked, "So how up to speed are ya?"

"Well I know that you saved me, *thanks again by the way,* and Annie told me that there's something going on but didn't tell me exactly what. Just that it's way bigger than what I was investigating."

"That it?"

"She also told me that almost everyone else on the planet thinks you're dead."

The lion nodded as he chewed the last bite of his breakfast. He swallowed and asked, "So why are you here?"

"Well, it's sort of a combination of helping my friend and a stranger who saved me, getting information to help get my job back, and a little bit of boredom." Paul laughed uncomfortably hoping his audience would too, but he didn't even chuckle. "The last part was a joke."

Unimpressed by the attempt at humor, the lion continued his interview, "What did Annie tell you about me?"

"She told me your name is Sampson Hart. Oh, I forgot to introduce myself." Paul stood up and reached out to shake hands. "I'm Paul Frost." The lion begrudgingly shook hands with the awkward penguin. "Um, so she told me your name and that you were the police chief and that you're dead.... well...that everyone thinks you're dead.... well everyone besides her."

The lion's one eye stared at Paul. "That's all you know? You don't know what you're getting yourself into, kid....but we could use the help. Okay, so here's the story..."

The first thing you need to know about DragonCorp is that when the company was founded nearly a hundred years ago, they were a defense contractor. Now, I don't mean that they made offensive weapons and marketed it as defense. I mean this company was in the business of keeping peace. Thomas Talon, the founder and the General's grandfather, believed in protecting people before anything else. They made missiles that knocked out enemy missiles and the best medical vehicles around. War has always been a part of life, but DragonCorp aimed to take the loss of life out of war. That worked for a while, but nations cared less and less about defense and more and more about having weapons that were bigger, faster, and stronger than their enemy's. DragonCorp nearly went bankrupt when the Board of Directors fired Thomas Talon. They replaced him with a young but decorated general, Thomas's grandson General Tobias Talon.

Under Tobias Talon's leadership, the company followed the trend of the world and began making offensive weapons, but DragonCorp didn't just make weapons; they made the biggest, baddest, most destructive ones you could imagine. The focus on saving lives transformed into a desire to make money at any cost.

But then something happened. New leaders began ruling countries—some overthrown, others voted into power—but these new heads of state paid attention to the destruction that was happening. What their predecessors were fighting for wasn't worth the price they were paying. Wars ended, and it left DragonCorp with another severe loss in sales.

That's when I first met General Talon. I had known of Talon by reputation only until he paid me a visit at our police station. He tried to sell his weapons to us, but I had no interest in them. Eagle City had its share of criminals, but our mission was to protect and serve, not seek and destroy.

Talon couldn't believe I said no. He lowered prices, offered incentives, and tried everything he could to get me to change my mind. None of it worked. I told him that his weapons were unnecessary. Just because we could be a dominant, fear-inducing force didn't mean we ought to be.

Almost immediately after that meeting, we noticed an increase in crime and also an increase in the firepower of the criminals. Purse snatchings turned into armed bank robberies; burglaries turned into hostage situations. I was never able to prove it, but I know Talon was behind it.

A few weeks later, Talon walked into the station again for another pitch. With the new demand that he had created, he was sure I'd change my mind, but I didn't waiver. He was shocked and furious with me. "You'll pay for this, Hart," he said as he left, and we never spoke again after that.

After that, a few things started happening. First, we started filling up our prison. It had been nearly vacant for years but with bigger crimes came longer times. Officers in my department began to turn on me. In the beginning, I assumed it was because I declined Talon's offers. Later, I'd find they were his newest employees and were caught up in the crimes they had been entrusted to stop. They'd soon join the other criminals in prison. Almost every week we'd catch several of Talon's goons, but for every one that we captured, it felt like two more replaced them. Our police force was tired, but we fought the good fight. Despite the long hours and hard work, we thwarted almost everything Talon tried. The only thing that caught me off guard was Lyla Pryde.

Lyla was the most beautiful tiger I had ever laid eyes on. We met at one of the mayor's fundraisers and hit it off right away. We went on several dates and spent time together whenever we could. I'm sure there were signs of what was to come, but I was blinded by love, and it nearly cost me my life.

It was a Friday night almost a year ago. I was waiting for Lyla to meet me at my apartment for dinner. The table was set with a bouquet of fresh flowers as the centerpiece. My place was on the second floor of a three-story complex, and she'd have to ring in to come up. Thinking maybe she'd rung and I hadn't heard her, I walked to the window that faced the entrance of the complex. I looked down and saw Lyla with two of my former officers holding DragonCorp weapons. They were in the same tactical formation the police force would use in a bank robbery to make sure the bandits wouldn't escape, and Lyla was clearly taking the lead. The window to my right suddenly shattered, and a stick of dynamite rolled on the floor toward me. I turned, but within a second, the blast sent me flying across the room. The heat of the blast burned my left eye, taking its sight. The force of the blast hurled me through the living room wall, and I landed at the foot of my bed. I heard another crash of glass to my left, then another blast. This time, a wall protected me but sent drywall and pieces of brick in my direction. I could barely stand but rose to my feet. Four more blasts went off at the ground level, and I could feel the integrity of the building begin to give way. I limped toward the bathroom; I had no chance at escaping, so I *tried to survive. With each step that I took, the floor fell behind me. I leapt for the tub. As I was airborne, the building collapsed, and I went into a free fall. I landed mostly in the tub. A pipe caught my right leg, and the force of the fall shattered my radius and ulna. I lied in that tub under a pile of rubble, but I was alive.*

I had to move. Surely, the foes had fled. With all my strength, I yanked my leg out of its trap and began to dig my way out. When I reached the surface, it felt like I was in a war zone. Thick, black smoke and dust were funneling up toward the sky—small patches at first that created more and more smoke. I had no one to trust and no place to go, so I hid. The dust and smoke were so thick I could barely see my nose. I hobbled on my good leg to a dumpster, and I pulled myself inside. As I did, I could hear the firetruck sirens and just make out the blue and red flashing lights. I closed the lid, sat down, and immediately blacked out from exhaustion.

When I woke hours later, it was dark. I didn't know what time, but it was late enough into the night, or early enough in the morning that almost everyone was asleep and off the streets. I crawled out and began walking. I didn't know where I'd go, but I didn't want to be found. I looked around but saw no sign of anyone. I crossed the street, and, once I got to the sidewalk, out of nowhere your friend Annie about knocked me over. She was walking home from the newspaper. She had reported on the fire and just finished her story. She took me in and cared for me as best she could.

She agreed to keep my survival a secret. Several people close to me had conspired to kill me. We didn't know who to trust. Annie wrote that my body was found and I was dead. There was a funeral, a gravestone, the whole nine yards. Only a few people know the truth, to the rest of the world...I'm dead.

Paul sat speechless and motionless. He stared through Sam. A single tear slid down his face. He stuttered, "In your apartment b-building...were there others li-living there?"

"There were...there was a gorilla on the top floor who lived but was injured pretty badly. Then there was an older couple who didn't make it out...two penguins."

Paul's single tear had turned into two steady streams flowing from his eyes. The penguin got up from the couch and went straight for the door. Sam let him go as he just realized Paul had lost much more than he had that day.

***

Paul sat on his couch. He stared at his television that wasn't on. It had been months since he thought about his parents' deaths. However, this was the first time he had heard they were murdered. Paul still had the voicemail on his phone. He played it.

Good evening, Mr. Frost. My name is Officer Cooper from the Eagle City Police Department. Um…I'm very sorry to tell you this, but there was an accident at your parents' apartment today. There was a gas main break at their home and…

Paul stopped the recording and set the phone on his end table. He continued to stare at the blank TV screen.

He sat and thought. Nearly a year had gone by, but the pain and sadness hit harder now than ever before. Thoughts in his head turned into audible words, and he began to talk to himself.

"They weren't unlucky. It wasn't chance. My parents were murdered!" he said with rage coursing through his body.

BZZZZZZZZT BZZZZZZZZT BZZZZZZZZT

His phone was ringing. Paul looked down to see "PRIVATE" on the Caller ID.

"Hello"

"Hey, kid, it's me, Sam. Hey uh…I didn't realize that you knew my neighbors…."

"TALON KILLED MY FAMILY," the penguin yelled, "AND THEN I WAS LIED TO AND TOLD IT WAS SOME FREAK ACCIDENT!" The tears had returned. He sniffled and regained some of his composure. "Those neighbors of yours were my mom and dad…"

"I'm sorry, Paul, I had no idea. Had I known I would have..."

What's the plan?" Paul suddenly changed the conversation's course.

"What?"

"The plan to take down Talon. I'm in. Whatever it looks like, I'm in."

***

General Talon stood with his back to his desk. His office was on the highest floor of the tallest tower in Eagle City. The sharply dressed Komodo dragon gazed through his window and over the land he wanted to rule so badly.

KNOCK KNOCK KNOCK

The door opened before a reply was given. Dr. Pigg entered and approached the general.

"Ah, good doctor, how are our plans moving along?"

"Very good, sir. The blueprints have been completed," Dr Pigg said as he rolled the plans open onto Talon's desk.

Talon scanned the document top to bottom, side to side, and over again. He looked at Dr. Pigg and gave a menacing smile. "Very good, Doctor, very good. And you have everything you need to begin production?"

"Not quite, sir," the pig retorted. "We will require some more materials. I know where our men can... *acquire* some, but we may need some more money as well."

"How much?"

Dr. Pigg handed over a small stack of papers. "Here is the scope of work, sir. A breakdown of everything my team will need is on the last page."

General Talon flipped through the stack, spending just a few seconds on each page.

"A case of bananas?" the confused general asked.

"For sustenance, sir. They are my favorite food"

The reptile gave a nod of understanding and continued through the paperwork. He spent the most time on the last page. When he finished, he gave another menacing grin and said, "Looks like we have a little shopping spree ahead of us."

The two laughed together, left the office, and began the next step toward Eagle City's destruction.

***

It was morning. Paul stood at the invisible door once again equipped with coffee and donuts. Like clockwork, the door opened the moment his watch struck 5 a.m.

Unlike his previous visits, Paul and Sam were not alone. Sam stood in the doorway. Behind him stood Annie and a German shepherd in police gear.

"Paul, I'd like you to meet Lieutenant Ricky Boone." The penguin shook hands with the dog. "Lieutenant Boone was my partner when I was an officer and my top lieutenant when I was Police Chief. He's about the only person on the force we can trust."

"Welcome to the team, kid" the dog said with a smirk as he opened the box of donuts and helped himself to a chocolate glazed.

The four gathered around the square kitchen table. Sam sat across from Paul, Annie between the two of them, and Boone stood with his back to a nearby wall.

"Okay, Paul," Sam started, "I just want to make sure you know what you're getting yourself into—"

"I'm in."

"This could get really dangerous. It—"

"I'm in."

"But General Talon—"

"Stop asking. I'm in."

Boone chuckled. "I like this kid. Where'd you find him, Hart? New recruit from the academy?"

"He's a sportswriter. And he found us," Sam replied.

Boone, who was mid-swig drinking his coffee, spit-sprayed it back into his cup. Sam shot his former partner a look that said, "I know," "Don't say anything," and "Trust me," all at once. The lieutenant remained silent.

The lion continued, "Now that everyone knows each other, let's get started. We've recently seen a spike in robberies all over the city." Sam placed three photographs of shady-looking characters on the table. "These three have been at the scene of every crime. They've also managed to *get away* every time as well. What we don't know is if they are escaping on their own or if some of Talon's moles in the police force are letting them go."

Paul picked up the photos. The first two criminals looked nearly identical—a pair of hyenas.

"Those are Hank and Henry Cackle. Twin brothers. A couple of petty crooks who started to work for Talon early on."

Paul flipped to the last photo. Sam spoke, "If you couldn't guess, it's..."

"Lyla," Paul finished. Even in a photo taken from a security camera, she was more beautiful than Sam had described.

The lion continued his briefing. "These three have robbed two jewelry stores and three banks in the last two nights. They aren't on the scene for long; they always trip the alarm, and they never get caught. At this point, there are only one jewelry store and one bank left that they haven't robbed. If they are going to strike again, it's going to be one of these two places, and, lucky for us, they are about three blocks away from each other. Boone will be out on patrol. Paul, you'll be rooftop lookout. Annie and I will be here monitoring the police scanners. Remember, this mission is about two things. Either catching Lyla and her two partners *or* finding out which officers are working for Talon. Either one of those outcomes is a victory for us."

The lion collected the mugshots and replaced the table space with a map of the city. He pointed at the map with each instruction.

"Boone, you'll be in your squad car patrolling this area. Paul, you'll be on the rooftop here. You'll have an earpiece to communicate with us, and this to help keep you hidden," Sam said as he directed his attention toward Lieutenant Boone. The dog was now holding a black jumpsuit.

Boone gently tossed the camouflage towards the penguin. "It's ultra lightweight, fire-resistant, made of a bulletproof material, and dry clean only," he said with a smirk.

Paul held up the uniform to compare its size with his own. Sam continued with the plan.

"We'll have binoculars for you tonight too. And Paul...I can't stress enough: You're a lookout. Boone will handle all the action. You're just his eyes in the sky."

Paul gave an affirming nod. The lion folded his map and packed it away. "Alright, team, go home and get some rest. We'll meet back here in twelve hours.

***

Paul sat on the rooftop's edge. He'd been there since before the bank closed just over five hours ago. Looking through his binoculars periodically, he waited for some sign of mischief. Paul had an unobstructed view of the bank's only entrance. Nobody was getting in or out without being seen.

Sam broke the string of radio silence. "You guys see anything?"

"Nothing here," Lieutenant Boone responded from his squad car walkie-talkie a few blocks away.

Just as Paul was ready to give a negative report, sirens and alarms went off inside the bank. "Guys, alarms are going off now. Boone, get here quick." Paul was completely surprised by the alarms. He'd been there for hours, and he knew without a doubt that he hadn't seen anyone go in through the bank's entrance.

Sam's voice cracked through the radio. "Good eye, Paul,

now STAY THERE! Do not pursue them!"

Paul half listened. While it wasn't a full pursuit, he moved closer to the action and began climbing down the fire escape to get a closer look.

The penguin could see the silhouette of three bandits each with bags of cash. This had to be Lyla and the two brothers.

They crossed the street, moving right toward Paul.

Lyla and the two brothers casually walked away from the bank until Boone's squad car careened around the corner. Spotlights on, red and blue lights flashing and siren blaring.

The bandits' casual walk transformed into a frantic run.

They darted for the alleyway where Paul stood above on the fire escape.

Paul had made his way to the last platform and still had not been detected by the bandits. Lyla and the two brothers ran single file right toward him. In a moment, Lyla would run right underneath his feet.

The penguin had an idea.

If he timed it right, Paul could release the sliding ladder and knock out one of the three crooks, ideally Lyla.

He unlatched the ladder, held it, and waited.

Lyla was twenty steps away.

Ten.

Five.

Paul released his grip.

In a flash, the tigress darted to her right. With lightning sharp reflexes, she narrowly avoided colliding with the ladder. Hank wasn't as skillful, or lucky, and ran face first into the steel rungs, immediately knocking him unconscious.

Henry, who was behind him, stopped to help.

"LEAVE HIM! LET'S GO!" Lyla screamed.

Henry grabbed Hank's bag of cash but quickly dropped it when he couldn't carry the weight.

Boone arrived on the scene and shined his flashlight on

the incapacitated hyena, then to the ladder, then up the ladder to Paul.

"Nice work, kid! I wasn't so sure about you, but...nice work!"

The penguin climbed down the ladder. Boone spoke into his walkie-talkie, "Boss, I'm not sure how you're going to react to this, but the kid just caught us one of the hyenas!"

"Super work, penguin. Nice job," Sam said over the group's radios.

"I gotta call this in," Boone responded. "Paul's headed back to you guys now. Sam, I'd get this kid some tools and get him doing a lot more than just being a look out."

The arrival of two squad cars abruptly ended the conversation. Paul quickly darted to the other end of the alleyway and disappeared into the night.

***

Super Citizen Stops Bank Burglar –Annie Freese
A bank was burglarized Wednesday night, and while the MO seemed all too familiar, this time a noble citizen intervened.

At 10 p.m. three masked individuals were seen leaving the First Frog Bank on the corner of Main and Vermilion with bags full of stolen bills. The three went west down an alley where an unnamed hero stepped in.

"I didn't see what happened," Lieutenant Richard Boone said. "We were in pursuit of the suspects. I followed them into the alleyway, and then all of the sudden one of the suspects is on the ground thanks to some help"

The "helper" was not able to be identified by Lieutenant Boone.

"He left as soon as I got to the scene. We don't know who he is but definitely appreciate the help......"

Sam stopped reading the story aloud to Annie and Paul. The three sat around the table of Sam's safe house. "Nice story Annie, and nice work 'Super Penguin.' Huh, that's got a nice ring to it. We should probably have a code name for you, so we stop using your name over the radio."

"So, remind me why we revealed what happened? Shouldn't we keep it a secret so Talon and his goons don't know what's going on?"

"Yeah...maybe." Sam chuckled. "But I like rubbing Talon's nose in it if we can. And the people need to hear about hope. The city's worse than it's ever been. Most of the police are crooked and hearing about a hero can't be a bad thing."

"I guess that makes sense. So, what's next?" Paul inquired.

"I'm glad you asked," answered the lion. "Follow me..." Sam opened a door that looked like a closet to reveal a ladder going to the second floor. The lion slowly climbed the ladder, and once he got to the top, Paul followed.

Just like the floor below, this level had been unkept with a few exceptions. The walls were covered in dust with cobwebs in each corner. Filling the room were various pieces of exercise equipment that weren't new, but seemed new to this space as their condition did not match the environment.

"Boone dropped these off for you to start training. The police station just got a whole new gym and didn't need these anymore."

Paul looked around the new set up. Free weights, a treadmill, and some other equipment that Paul didn't quite recognize were lined up against the wall leading to a makeshift boxing ring. "Ok, Sam...what the heck is all this for?"

"Well, son, if you're going to be on the front lines of this thing, you're going to want to know how to fight. What kind of experience do you have?

Paul's face showed confusion, and slight embarrassment. "Did you just ask me what kind of fighting experience I have? I'm a sportswriter for goodness sake..."

"Right....but you've done something, right? Wrestling in high school? A self-defense class? Anything?"

Paul shook his head.

"Alright," Sam replied as he ducked between the ropes and hobbled into the ring. "Now's as good a time as ever!"

Paul stared. "Right now? Are you serious?"

"Yeah, let's see what you've got!"

"I'm pretty confused right now Sam... Just last night my orders were 'Stay away. Don't get involved.' Now you want me to train because I disobeyed that?"

The lion responded, "I like to think of your insubordination as more of a try-out." He chuckled. "You showed us last night that you're willing to put yourself in harm's way for this town. Lord knows we need the help, and if you're able and willing, we've got work for you."

"I'm not a soldier or hero or whatever you're thinking. I'm a writer. Last night was just a knee-jerk reaction."

"I didn't know penguins had knees." Sam laughed at his own joke despite Paul's unamused glance. The lion stopped laughing, collected himself, and continued, "Look, Paul, you proved last night that when you see something wrong, you're willing to try and do good. That's all it takes to be a hero. You don't need to be comfortable with it; you just have to be willing to do it when the time comes. We'll start small by cleaning up the streets with some of these petty crimes and work our way up to Talon. Whaddya think?"

"You really think I can do this?"

"I know you can, kid, but that doesn't matter. Annie and Boone, they know you can too, but to be totally honest, that doesn't matter either. The only person who needs to think you can be great is you. You can be unstoppable if you believe in yourself, and if you don't think you can do it...well then I guess we've already failed."

Paul smiled. "Alright, old man, don't start getting emotional on me." The penguin approached the ring and slid under the ropes. Sam towered over him. "This is a terrible idea by the way, but here we are."

"There's a bo staff in that corner behind you. Grab it."

Paul obeyed. He turned his back to the lion, walked toward the wooden staff, bent over and *SWOOSH*. Sam had swung a staff of his own at Paul's legs, knocking the penguin on his back. "Rule Number One. Never turn your back on your opponent."

The penguin snarled inaudibly, and, with his eyes on Sam picked up his staff again.

"You're a little guy, Paul. You're going to have to rely on weapons and technique to take down bigger foes. Paul nodded and Sam continued his lesson. "First, I want you to practice using the staff. Try different grips, different ways of swinging it. Get familiar with your tool."

Paul followed the command. He swung the staff with one hand, two hands, and even twirled it around like a helicopter propeller.

"Alright, Paul, now I'm going to attack. I want you to block."

On the first attack, Sam swung his staff overhead, and Paul blocked successfully. Next, Sam swung from the side, and Paul blocked again. On the third attack, Sam swung from his right, which was quickly blocked by Paul, but then Sam thrusted his back hand, and the other end of the staff whomped Paul on the side of the head. "Oh!" exclaimed Paul.

"You didn't expect me to go easy on you, did you?"

"Bring it, old man!" The two continued to spar this way. Paul blocked a majority of the strikes, but every few attempts ended with a *WHOMP* to the head or torso of the penguin.

"Alright, now I want you to attack, and I'll block."

"Seriously? We've been doing this for hours, Sam. I need a break."

"As soon as you hit me once, we'll be done for the day."

Paul's face lit up. "Deal!" The penguin took a moment to

stretch and loosen his muscles. He did the helicopter spin a few times and was ready.

Paul struck overhead.

BLOCKED.

Swipe from the left.

BLOCKED.

Fake overhead and swipe right.

BLOCKED.

Sam smiled. "You gotta be quicker than that, kid."

Swipe.

BLOCK.

Swipe.

BLOCK.

This went on and on for several minutes.

Paul looked past Sam toward the entryway and waved. "Hey, Annie, what are you up to?"

Sam turned around for just a moment and *BAM!*

Paul struck the lion in the back of the head with a swiping strike, knocking him face first to the ground.

Sam rolled onto his back and laughed. "Kind of a cheap shot, don't you think?"

"Rule Number One," Paul responded as he extended a flipper to pull the lion to his feet.

"Ha ha, not a bad first day, kid. Same time tomorrow."

Paul continued to train. From hand-to-hand combat to wrestling techniques, each day had a different lesson. After several lessons, bumps, and bruises, Paul started to show great improvement. He had become more visibly fit. While he wasn't *buff,* the penguin had dropped some weight and started to have some muscle definition under his feathers.

A month had passed since the night on the rooftop. Paul entered the base at 5 a.m. on the dot just as he always did. When he entered Annie was already there. They were both waiting for his arrival. "Good morning." He examined their odd expressions. "So uh....what's the plan for today?"

"We've got presents!" Annie exclaimed. She clapped her paws together bursting with excitement.

The lion limped to his closet a few feet away and pulled out a black duffle bag with the Eagle City Police logo on it. "Boone dropped this off for you after last night's training session."

The lion opened the bag and began removing its contents.

"If you're going to be this city's hero, you're going to need some tools. Just in case there's not a fire escape around," Sam said with a smirk and a glance from his good eye.

The lion first pulled out a four-foot long baton. The long, cylindrical weapon was flat on one end, while the other end had two prongs. "This will be your main weapon. It's metal, so it's a little bit stronger than the staff you've been using in training. We aren't planning to use lethal force, but our enemies won't be so cordial. Use this for physical contact, and if necessary...." Sam twisted the baton at its center. A bolt of steady electricity flowed between the two prongs ".... zap the heck out of 'em. And for convenience, it's collapsible." Sam demonstrated as the pole slid into itself and shrank to about a foot in length.

He reached into the bag again and pulled out three hand-held orbs. "These are smoke bombs. If you get into a situation and need a way out, push this red button on the side, toss it, and run."

He dug into the bag one last time and pulled out a large, red piece of fabric.

"This is something Boone and Annie rigged up for you. The outside is bulletproof Kevlar, while the inside is made from old parachutes, so you wear it around your neck. It can be a shield or a glider for you depending on the..."

"It's a cape," Paul stated.

Annie corrected, "No, it's a multi-functional—"

Sam and Paul interrupted in unison, "It's a cape."

With defeat in her voice, Annie called back, "It's a cape."

The three laughed before Sam brought back the focus. "Alright, Super Penguin, you're ready for the field. Time for your first mission."

***

A few weeks later...

"Super Penguin Strikes Again" by Annie Freese

Two more bank robberies were thwarted this week by our city's protector Super Penguin.

"He's been a huge help for us around the city," Lieutenant Richard Boone said. "That's the tenth bank robbery that's been stopped thanks to Super Penguin. When you tally up all the crimes he's helped stop, his resume is pretty impressive."

The city's mysterious protector had previously stopped or caught criminals in nine bank robberies and three jewelry store thefts. Super Penguin even prevented a group of crooks from stealing the world's largest diamond from its home at the Eagle City Art & History Museum.

Super Penguin may have only been here for a few weeks now, but he has certainly left an impression on Eagle City's citizens.

General Talon wadded the newspaper into a ball and chucked it against the wall. Dr. Pigg, Lyla, and Henry stood warily in his office. "Seriously? If this penguin messes up one more thing," the giant lizard roared. He stood behind his desk, put both his hands down, and dug his claws into the wooden desk. "I need him gone. Whatever it takes, I want him out of the picture. Do I make myself clear?" The three nodded.

"Lyla and Henry," Talon began delegating. "Go find him and bring him to me. By whatever means necessary"

The two nodded again.

"GO! NOW!" he screamed as he dug his claws even further into the desk.

The tiger and hyena jumped and darted out the door.

The Komodo dragon let out a sigh of frustration. "Dr, Pigg, where are we on your project?"

"Well, sir, as you know, we have had multiple setbacks...."

"No excuses, Pigg, and don't bring up that bird. So help me if you say a word about that bird..."

"Very sorry, General. We've fully produced a little more than fifty percent of your requested amount."

"So, we have five hundred ready to go?"

"Yes, sir. They need to go through a training simulator for the AI, but once that is complete, your army will be ready."

"Excellent," he said with a menacing scowl. "Most excellent."

***

Paul read the same newspaper article with Annie miles away at Tina's Diner.

"Very nice article, Annie. Thanks to this 'Super Penguin,' it looks like your career is finally taking off!" Paul joked.

"Thanks, jerk," she jabbed back. "By the way, congratulations on coming back from suspension. I just heard tomorrow is your first day back. Why didn't you tell me?"

"Yeah, thanks. Myles was *officially caught* which was enough evidence for Trunk Senior to think I'm an asset! Ha! To be honest, if it weren't for my bills, I probably wouldn't have come back. I've been kinda busy, you know."

"So, what you're saying is...you won't be there for long?"

Unbeknownst to the two friends, Henry and Lyla patiently waited outside in an unmarked, panel van.

"Do you really think that's the penguin?" The hyena, in the driver's seat, asked his partner. They had just left DragonCorp to begin their hunt for Super Penguin. "We just started looking. I mean, there's hundreds of penguins in the city. Are we really going to stake out the first one we come across?"

"Shut up!" Lyla responded while looking through a pair of binoculars. "The bear he's with is the reporter doing the stories about the bird. Looking at this penguin, I doubt he's *Mr. Hero,* but I think the bear is our lead."

The hyena remained silent.

Inside, the penguin and polar bear had finished their dinners. They paid their bill at the counter and made their way through the exit. The pair walked toward their cars while the hyena and tiger waited to pounce. Lyla was equipped with a pair of nun-chucks while Henry preferred his wooden bat. Both held their weapons while they waited.

"NOW!" Lyla shouted to Henry. The duo sprang from their van and ran towards their targets. Once Lyla was in striking distance, she whacked Paul with her nun-chucks, nailing him with a brutal *BOP* in the back of his head. The force of the blow knocked him to the ground. With one hit, the penguin was knocked unconscious. Henry swung his bat at Annie's abdomen. The polar bear caught the bat with one hand. She let out a ferocious roar. Lifting the bat in the air, and Henry with it, Annie swung the hyena at Lyla where he landed on top of his partner. Lyla shoved Henry off her, got up, and ran at Annie.

Annie swung.

Lyla ducked and swung her nun-chuck, striking Annie in the back,

Annie stumbled forward.

Lyla swung overhead as she took a step toward the bear.

Annie planted on her left foot and gave a relentless right kick straight into Lyla's gut. The tiger flew several feet into a light post.

While the two women squared off, Henry snuck back into the van.

Lyla rose to her feet, wiped sweat from her forehead, and charged toward Annie again.

Annie waited for the attack, and when the tiger got close enough, the bear punched.

Lyla slid underneath the strike.

The tiger tried her attack again, but Annie was ready.

Before Lyla could strike, Annie had spun and thrown a powerful punch right in the tiger's torso.

Lyla went airborne again, this time crashing into the windshield of her van.

The tiger pulled herself out of the broken windshield and spun off the hood onto the ground. Her partner scooped her up, set her into the back of the van, and quickly drove away.

By now, Paul regained consciousness. He looked around confused. "Wh-what happened?"

"Lyla Pryde and the other hyena brother."

"How did they know?"

"I don't think they do," Annie pondered while she spoke. "They didn't seem very interested in you, Paul. I think they were here for me...head back to base quick."

"Wait, why just me? What about you?"

"You need to get out of here. Between Sam and Trunk, you have two bosses who don't want you involved in any kind of police investigation. The cops will be here soon. I can handle this." Annie nodded, telling him to leave.

"Alright, if you say so." The penguin dusted himself, got into his car, and drove away.

***

General Talon stood in his office alone. He stared out his window looking out over Eagle City.

KNOCK KNOCK KNOCK

The general turned. "Come in." His guests were Lyla and Henry. "I hope you have good news to report. I fired the last two people who came in to tell me about their failures."

"No, sir," Lyla spoke up. She cleared her throat. "We too have failed you once again. We found the reporter, the bear who has been doing the reports on Super Penguin. She was just down the road at a diner with a penguin."

"And?" General Talon asked.

"Not the penguin we were looking for," Henry joined in the conversation. "Lyla knocked him out rather easily. I think he was just another reporter."

"So, we have him in custody, I presume. Do we have the bear too?"

"No, sir," Lyla answered. "We weren't expecting the bear to put up much of a fight.... but we were wrong."

"She took down the both of you?"

"Yes, sir." Lyla hung her head. "The bear was very strong. I think if we—"

"Forget about the bear," Talon cut her off. "I only want the penguin!"

"Yes, sir, " Lyla replied. "If we must bring in every penguin in town, we'll do whatever it takes to find him."

"Yes, do that!"

Confused, Henry asked, "Do what?"

"Bring in every penguin," Talon said matter-of-factly. "The mayor owes me a favor or two. The chief of police too. We create a story about 'bringing the vigilante to justice' or something and bring in every penguin until we figure out who he is. Thank you for the idea, Lyla. Oh, and Henry, Dr. Pigg is going to need your assistance down in his lab. Please hurry."

"Will do, boss." The hyena left immediately.

Confused, Lyla thought for a moment and asked, "What's he doing? Should I go with him?"

"Not if you want to live," Talon said with a menacing grin. "Depending on how the roundup goes, you may be needed for a future test. It would be in your best interest to not fail me again."

***

Henry walked to Dr. Pigg's office. The lights were on, and the door was open, so he walked right in.

"Hey, Doc, are you in here?"

No response.

Henry continued through the office. Dr. Pigg wasn't there. The office overlooked a huge, indoor testing sight. It was an incredibly large room two stories tall and the size of a football field, used to test DragonCorp's newest weapons. The room was mostly empty except for a few areas with crates and equipment. Henry left the office, went downstairs, and wandered into the middle of the testing room, peering around the boxes. "Doc...you down here?"

Suddenly, every door in the room slammed shut in unison.

With a loud *CLUNK* of the doors' deadbolts, two spotlights lit up facing Henry. A voice came over the loudspeaker.

"Well hello, Mr. Cackle."

"Doc... what's going on?"

"Oh, Mr. Cackle, don't worry. This session should be quicker and less painful than the previous tests."

"Wh...what?"

"Oh splendid, the General didn't tell you?" The pig laughed in delight. "And they said Talon didn't like to have fun. One moment, let me add that to my notes. *Subject...unaware of.... research.* Okay then, Mr. Cackle, we are all set. Good luck!" Dr. Pigg chuckled as he turned off the microphone. The swine sat back in his chair, grabbed a banana, and eagerly watched his experiment unfold.

The room was silent.

Then, all light disappeared.

Pitch black.

Henry dropped to the ground and began to blindly crawl searching for a hiding space. He didn't know what was coming, but he knew it couldn't be good. The hyena felt a large wooden crate and leaned against it.

Several yards away, a bright, red light began to flash, and with it came the sound of a garage door opening. When the noise stopped so did the light. Next came the sound of unnatural marching, perfectly in sync, steel feet clanging on concrete floor.

The sound grew louder and louder as the mysterious beings got closer. Henry peered around the corner, and he saw five red lights shining. Beneath it he could make out an antenna connected to each flashing light. The glow of the red lights shined just brightly enough to make out a robotic face. Dr. Pigg's project was a robot army, and Henry was the target.

As he had this realization, the middle robot locked eyes with him. It raised its right arm, and a spring-loaded gun popped out of the forearm, shooting a laser beam from the end of it. Henry sprang back to his box. The laser followed and cut the wooden crate in half, setting it ablaze.

The clanging feet broke into a run coming right for him.

Henry searched frantically for more cover. He crawled several yards and stopped when he felt a smooth, pipe-like, metal surface. The hyena felt his way upward and found a large, steel box.

The red lights had disappeared without him noticing. Henry looked around, and, before he knew what happened, a red light lit inches from his face.

The robot lifted its left arm.

Another spring-loaded gun, but this time a stream of electricity shot out.

The voltage was so strong, the hyena couldn't control his body. This went on for several seconds.

Henry's eyes rolled into the back of his head.

When it finally stopped, Henry immediately collapsed to the floor in a heap. Smoke rose from his body.

Overhead the lights turned back on. Two robots each grabbed one of the hyena's legs and dragged away his motionless body.

***

Today was Paul's first day back at work. He didn't have to re-port to Sam at 5 a.m., so he slept in for a few extra hours. His routine was disturbed, and there was an eerie vibe returning to the *Eagle City Inquirer*. Only a few months had passed, but so much had changed.

After he completed his morning routine, Paul sat at the edge of his bed and packed his backpack with work supplies. The penguin tossed his bag across his shoulder, grabbed his keys, and went out the door.

The door suddenly re-opened. "Almost forgot it!" Paul said as he reentered his home and grabbed his new voice recorder, a welcome back gift from Annie. He put the recorder into his side pocket.

Paul got into his car and drove to work. When he arrived at the parking garage next to the *Inquirer*, his unofficial park-ing space was taken. It was his no-good work nemesis Howie. The penguin let out an annoyed sigh and moved up to the top level of the garage. As he parked, his phone vibrated.

It was from Annie, "Welcome back to the newsroom!"

Paul replied, "Thanks! Did you plan me a welcome back party?"

"LOL! I'm still shocked Trunk let you back!

"Me too, but I'm glad to be back. Even though that darn duck Howie took my parking place!!! I'll lay low I promise. Do you work today?"

"I'm off today, planning some things with Sam. Come by after work."

"Sounds good. See ya then!"

Paul sent his last text as he walked to the front door of the *Inquirer*. His entrance was identical to his first day. Few heads rose to even notice him, and the ones that did sent an unemo-tional glance. He got one smile and nod from Tony, a tiger, who worked in advertising.

When the penguin got to his desk, it was barren and empty, covered in duct tape and glue residue from repair attempts since Trunk's rampage. "Ah, home sweet home," he said to an audience of none. Paul unpacked his backpack and began to settle in.

Once his final pen was in its place and everything was transferred from his bag to his desk, Paul sat and reflected. Everything at the newsroom was the same as when he left, yet it felt bizarre and foreign. Paul's life had turned upside down, and now he was trying to go back to "normal." The penguin twirled his pen and pulled out the Egret's schedule to begin work, but as he did that, five shadows were cast from behind him.

Paul slowly twirled around in his chair. There stood Mr. Trunk, Lieutenant Boone and three other police officers he didn't know. Howie stood not far behind. "QUACK!" Paul and his visitors all looked Howie's way. "Sorry," he whispered and walked away from the scene.

"Mr. Frost," Lieutenant Boone said as if the two had never met, "by order of Mayor Mooney, all penguins in Eagle City are being detained and questioned regarding the vigilante Super Penguin and his misconduct."

"What?" Paul was exasperated. He looked at his friend Boone. "What's going on? Do I have any choice?"

"No, sir, the directive from the mayor and police chief is to collect all penguins. We will give you the option to come willingly or be arrested and charged with *interfering in a police investigation*."

"And I have to go right now? I mean, I literally just started working a few minutes ago," Paul said as he glanced at his boss. This was the first time he'd seen a look of sympathy from Tom Trunk.

"No, sir, the directive from the mayor and police chief are that all penguins will be notified and collected immediately.

We have spoken with your employer. He is very understanding of the situation, and, with your cooperation, we can return you to your work as soon as possible."

"Well, I guess if I have no choice." The penguin stood from his chair. Every eye in the room was focused on this interaction. Some tried to hide it, while others made it obvious they were watching. Trunk attempted to get his staff to settle down but was mostly unsuccessful. Paul heard another obnoxious, yet uncontrollable "QUACK!" from Howie as he walked out of the newsroom.

When he got outside, there were two squad cars. The first car had three penguins in the back already; the second car was empty. When Boone got in the first car and he was being led to the second, Paul realized that he wouldn't have the opportunity to talk to his friend at all.

Paul was directed into the back seat of the squad car, and the door was closed behind him.

Two officers settled into their seats. The driver turned to his partner and spoke as if Paul wasn't there. "Boss says this was the last one." The passenger nodded his head in agreement.

Paul interjected, "So, can you guys at least tell me where you're taking me?"

The driver turned his head to Paul and answered, "DragonCorp."

***

"They are all here, sir," Lyla said as she approached General Talon in his office.

"Every penguin in Eagle City? I'm impressed. That was much quicker than I thought it would be. How many are there?"

"We have 253, sir"

"Hmm, the census I had said 251. Let me see the report."

Lyla handed it over, and Talon flipped through the pages. He leaned toward Lyla and pointed. "Ah, here...these two are puffins. They can go." The general handed the report back to her. "Have we had any hero type reveal himself?"

"No, sir."

"No uproars, signs of protest, suspicious whispering?"

"No, sir. Everyone is scared but cooperating."

"Hmm." The general paused to take in the information. "Tell Dr. Pigg I'll be right down."

"Will do, sir," Lyla replied. She left the room and headed to the auditorium. It was a few minutes' walk from Talon's office. When she arrived, she entered from the back of the room. The auditorium was full of frantic penguins in nearly every seat. Young, old, male, female, it didn't matter; if they were a penguin, they were there. Across the front of the stage stood six armed police officers spaced apart evenly.

Lyla walked through the aisle and across the front row. On stage right, there was a small wooden staircase that led onto the stage. She walked up it and approached Dr. Pigg who stood in the center, behind a podium, watching the penguins.

"The General is on his way."

Dr. Pigg ignored her statement and moved immediately to another conversation. "The General only wanted Super Penguin, but I have so many more tests to run. I could use this whole room if he would let me..." He grinned manically and rubbed his hands together.

Lyla looked puzzled, but before she could respond, General Talon walked in from the backstage door. He walked right past his subordinates and toward the podium. Dr. Pigg moved out of his way, and Talon spoke to his audience.

"Welcome, my guests, welcome," he said with an artificial smile. "You, no doubt, must be wondering why you're here, so I'll get straight to the point. Our precious city has been invaded by a vigilante—a penguin vigilante. Someone who has no regard for the law and has decided to take the rules into his own hands. As you know, this kind of behavior is not only dangerous but highly, highly illegal. We are but a host to the mayor and police department's investigation. Officers will be interviewing you each one by one, and once we find our little rule breaker, you'll all be free to go." He finished with the same smile with which he had begun his speech.

Paul sat and listened. He was stuck, but he had some time. The interrogation line began at the front row on the far left. He sat about fifty people away from that point, but sooner or later his time would come. He thought to himself, "Is there any way to fight my way out?" He felt in his pockets. Nothing but a paper notepad and his recorder. Not even a pencil to use for a weapon. With six armed officers and a countless number of Talon's goons surrounding the facility, fighting his way out wasn't going to work.

Suddenly, Talon returned to the stage and approached the microphone. Following behind him were two police officers restraining a penguin who couldn't budge.

"Good news, everyone. As luck would have it, our first interview was also our only interview. This penguin here has confessed to everything and revealed himself to be the criminal Super Penguin." Talon gave his maniacal grin again. "Take him to the back boys."

"NO!" the penguin cried out. "It's not me. You've got the wrong peng—" His beak was muffled by Lyla.

In the front row, a female penguin with two young penguins by her side also became frantic, screaming, "It's not him! He's not Super Penguin!" while her two children cried.

While his henchmen wrestled the penguin, General Talon addressed his audience again. "You will all be released shortly. Please take a seat. Most of the crowd listened, everyone except Paul.

"Wait!" he exclaimed now standing in the center aisle. Talon paused, and his menacing grin returned. "That's not Super Penguin!" Every eye in the auditorium was on Paul.

Talon returned to the podium. "And how do you know this?"

"Because..." he paused for a moment, still unsure of the right move to make. He may have been able to go free and fight another day, but he couldn't let an innocent penguin pay for his silence. "Because I'm Super Penguin!"

A collective gasp filled the room. General Talon stood silently as his grin grew in size and severity. His trap had worked.

Without direction, two officers, both dalmatians, grabbed Paul from behind. He didn't struggle and walked with the guards.

The two police officers led Paul onto the stage in front of Talon while the other accused penguin stood next to him. General Talon sized them both up and said, "Hmm, I'm not sure either of you are Super Penguin..." Talon turned away and began to leave. As he did, he said in front of the crowd, "Kill them both."

The officers raised their guns.

Paul reacted instinctively with a hard elbow into the left guard's midsection. When he hunched forward, Paul used that momentum, flipping the guard and slamming him onto the wood floor. Then, Paul swept his leg under the second officer, knocking him off his feet and onto his back. He did this seemingly all in one motion. Both guards rolled on the floor in pain.

"Ah, Super Penguin, we finally meet!" Talon pulled out a handgun, aimed it at the penguin's midsection, and fired.

Direct hit to the chest. Paul felt a sudden sting. He looked down and a dart stuck out of his shirt. The penguin started to feel dizzy, and seconds later, he collapsed into an unconscious heap on the floor.

"Take him to my office," Talon ordered, and two officers picked him up. One grabbed ahold of Paul's legs, the other holding his flippers.

"General Talon," Dr. Pigg asked as he approached. "What

should we do with the others? I have some more experi...."

"Whatever you'd like, Dr. Pigg, but keep the testing site clear for now. We may need it for my friend here."

***

Annie sat at Sam's kitchen table, flipping through some cold case files she believed were linked to DragonCorp. Suddenly, her cell phone rang. The Caller ID read *"Restricted."*

"Hello?"

"Is this Annie Freese?"

"Umm, can I ask who's calling?" She tilted her head in confusion.

"If this is Annie Freese, you need to get down to Dragon-Corp now. Your penguin friend needs help."

"What? Who is this? What's happening at DragonCorp?" Annie was now standing.

"You need to get here now! I will lead you to him when you get here. Bring anyone you trust." The conversation abruptly ended.

Annie briskly walked into the next room where Sam was tinkering with some tools. "Paul's in trouble. We gotta go!"

***

Paul opened his eyes. A large room...big desk...expensive-looking artwork on the walls. Despite having never seen it, Paul accurately assumed he was in Talon's office. As he came to, the next thing Paul realized was that he was tied to his chair. He struggled, but his flippers didn't budge.

"Sir, the penguin is awake," said an unknown voice a few feet behind Paul. The voice was followed by the *krrrr* of a walkie-talkie. The voice didn't make another sound.

Paul looked around the room for a way to escape. While he scanned the room, he saw a familiar-looking pile with his recorder and notepad neatly displayed.

After a few minutes of struggle and silence, distant footsteps could be heard coming closer. The door opened, and General Talon passed through. Two armed guards followed and stood at either side of him. Talon sat down at his desk and stared into the eyes of the penguin.

The giant lizard gave his signature, menacing grin.

"Untie him," General Talon ordered. "And if he tries anything, shoot to kill."

The guard to Talon's left obeyed. Once free, Paul glanced behind him. A dozen more armed DragonCorp guards stood watch.

"There's more in the hallway, Paul, so, if you try anything, you *will* die."

The penguin turned back around to face the General.

"Where are the others? All those penguins you kidnapped?"

"Mr. Frost, was it?" General Talon asked. "They are all still here in a secure location. Their safety and your cooperation go hand in hand. In other words, all of you get to go home today, or we no longer have penguins in Eagle City. Do I make myself clear?"

Paul nodded in affirmation.

Talon glanced at the penguin's belongings on the edge of the desk. He gave another order, "Give Mr. Frost his belongings. There's nothing here he can cause any trouble with, and I don't like it on my desk."

The guard followed the orders and returned Paul's things to him. Paul put them into his pockets.

"Mr. Frost, do you know why you're here? Why I didn't just kill you?"

"Permission to stand, sir?" Paul asked unexpectedly.

"Excuse me?"

"I've been sitting here for a while and was sitting in the auditorium. My legs are falling asleep, and I'm a little uncomfortable is all."

Talon snickered. "Of course, Mr. Frost, that will be fine."

Paul stood and put his flippers in his pocket.

"Well, Mr. Frost? Do you know why you're still alive?"

Paul didn't answer and just stared.

"Ah, playing hard to get, are we? Well, Mr. Frost. I'll come right out and say it. You have a gift. Your combat skills, intellect, and abilities are all top notch. But you've also been a major thorn in my side. I don't like that, but I also don't like the idea of wasting an opportunity to *hire* an excellent candidate as yourself to join me."

"Join you for what, exactly?"

"I'm sure you already know, little bird, but in case you didn't, DragonCorp owns this city! The mayor, the chief of police, and most of the force. Anyone with any real power in this city reports to ME! We started with Eagle City. That's almost complete, and we are one step closer to controlling the world! The whole world under one ruler, and I, the KING!" Talon's sharp, white teeth shimmered as he smiled his insane smile. "Now, I'll ask you one more time bird, are you with us, or are you dying today?"

Paul opened his mouth to respond, but before any words came out, Lyla came storming into the room.

"GENERAL! THE PRISONERS ARE GONE!"

Talon, with all his might, pounded two fists onto the desk. A humungous thud rang out. "WHAT HAPPENED?"

"Well, sir," Lyla spoke nervously, "with all our security detail here, there was a breach."

"Someone broke in?"

"Not exactly, sir. Henry Cackle, my ex-partner..."

The General interrupted, "Yes...the colossal failure, Dr. Pigg used him as a test subject. He's dead."

"Again, not exactly, sir." Lyla was uncharacteristically nervous and trembling. "He survived the test. We aren't sure how. His body went unaccounted for, and we assumed it was a filing error. But...Dr. Pigg pulled up the security footage. He's alive, and they all just escaped."

Talon pounded the desk harder than before, and this time, the room shook. The General glared at Paul who had a big, satisfied grin on his face. He didn't have to say a word, and Talon knew the offer was declined. Talon picked up his desk phone and punched in Dr. Pigg's number.

"General, I deeply apologize, sir I—"

"We are bringing Super Penguin to you now. Get the test site ready." Talon hung up the phone before Pigg could respond. He looked at the guard to his left. "Tie him back up. It's *showtime.*"

***

Paul rose to his feet. With an armed guard in every direction, they made their way to and through a door. General Talon walked a few paces behind with more guards behind him. They walked this way until they reached Dr. Pigg's laboratory that overlooked the weapons testing room. Paul was ushered to the front and overlooked the room. Below were nearly 500 robots.

Roughly 100 of them stood at one end of the room. These were a dark grey color with a box head and a red bulb at the end of a long antenna. The other 400 were sleeker and more polished. They were a glossy white color, with a blue Dragon-Corp logo stamped on their chests. No unsightly antenna could be seen, and the robots looked much more advanced.

Talon moved through the crowd of guards and stood beside Paul.

"Mr. Frost, I'd like to share with you my master plan. You've been a worthwhile adversary despite being a royal pain in my tail, and before you die, I want you to know exactly how we beat you, no, *destroyed* you and your precious city."

Talon grinned his evil grin.

"To the left there, you'll see Phase 1." Talon pointed to the 100 less impressive robots. "The Phase 1 robots go into Eagle City with one mission: Destroy everything they can. Buildings, roads, citizens—whatever they come across. The police will try to stop them. Officers that don't work for me will likely die, and those that are employed by me will know to stay out of the way."

Paul looked on in disgust.

"And then we have Phase 2." He motioned to the other 400 bots. "These are your replacements Super Penguin. These robots, publicly made by DragonCorp, will swoop in and save the day. *Then*, after the police force is half wiped out and half proven to be incompetent, my robotic minions will replace them. I really don't know why I didn't think of this sooner. Instead of bribing and hiring an army, we BUILT one! And the best part is, the stupid citizens of Eagle City won't even know they've been invaded. Instead of conquering the world with fear and force, we are going to do it by tricking these fools into thinking they are safe! One last chance, Mr. Frost. Is Super Penguin going to join with DragonCorp?"

"Never!"

"Then you leave me no choice. Doctor, send about fifty bots out to start Phase 1." Dr. Pigg nodded. "Then, send the penguin down there for a final test of the rest of the bots. Make it quick, and try not to make a mess."

***

Talon left to watch the havoc he had unleashed on the city. Dr. Pigg stood in his lab overlooking the DragonCorp soldiers getting Paul into position. One guard began to untie the knot holding the penguin's flippers together.

POW! WHAM! BAM!

As soon as he was free, Paul unleashed a flurry of punches and kicks onto the guards.

Outnumbered, Paul was quickly on the receiving end of the guards' kicks and punches. The penguin fell to the floor.

"That's enough, gentlemen. Leave something for the test." Dr. Pigg said over the loud-speaker, and the guards left the room. Paul stumbled to his feet beaten and bruised.

A circle had formed around him made up of robots.

The penguin clinched his flippers and snarled.

All of the robots were initially offline, but one by one, and at a hasty pace, the red bulb at the end of the antenna on their heads began to light, showing they were activated.

Paul stood now surrounded by fifty robots with their only objective being to kill him.

The circle began to shrink as the robots closed in on Paul. The space grew smaller and smaller.

A bot from behind the penguin grabbed his shoulder.

Paul grabbed the robot's arm and with all his strength ripped it out of its socket.

Sparks flew, and, in one motion, the penguin swung the detached arm, knocking its owner to the ground.

Then he swung the arm at the two closest bots stumbling them backwards.

Just as he did this, two more bots each grabbed one of Paul's flippers from behind.

He struggled to no avail.

One more bot approached, wound up to throw a massive punch, and...

ZAP!

A laser beam, shot from the direction of Dr. Pigg's lab, blasted a hole in the attacking robot's head. It fell into a heap on the floor.

ZAP!!! ZAP!!! ZAP!!!

Now steady streams of lasers were firing from multiple points, all coming from the lab.

Bot after bot fell. Every Phase 1 bot was either out of the

building or now in a smoldering heap.

Once the smoke cleared, Paul looked up to Dr. Pigg's laboratory. The glass window was shattered and smoking. Inside, there were no soldiers and no Dr. Pigg. Instead, Paul saw his friend Annie with the hyena, Henry Cackle, both holding incredibly large firearms that were emitting smoke from their ends.

"Here. You'll need this," Annie said, and she tossed Paul his Super Penguin uniform. "Hurry up and get that on. We've got a city to save."

***

Paul followed Annie and Henry through the halls of Dragon-Corp. Incapacitated guards were everywhere. While most were unconscious, a few slowly crawled in pain. Paul gazed upon the scene confused.

"That was all her," Henry said as he pointed in Annie's direction. Paul smirked but remained silent, still unsure of the situation. Just a few days ago, the hyena in front of him had jumped him and his friend. Now they were working together.

Annie continued to lead the group past her trail of knocked out foes until they reached an exterior door. As the polar bear walked through the door, a white panel van approached with Sam in the driver's seat.

The lion sped toward them and suddenly screeched to a halt. With a grin, Sam began to brag, "I might only have one eye, but..." Mid-sentence he noticed the hyena. Sam's tone suddenly became alert and concerned, "What's he doing here?"

"I'll explain on the way," answered Super Penguin, "but he's with us now. We need to get downtown. NOW!"

The bear, hyena, and penguin filed into the back of the van. They sat down and buckled their seatbelts as Sam sped off.

"Henry was the mystery caller, Sam." Annie then looked at Paul. "If it weren't for Henry, we would have had no idea you were here much less that you were in trouble."

Sam glared at Henry. "But why is he with us now? How do we know this isn't some part of Talon's plan?"

Henry interrupted, "Okay guys, first off, I'm right here." He waved sarcastically and smirked. "Secondly, Talon wanted Super Penguin, and he got him. Any planning Talon did regarding this crew ended with the penguin being left in that room and then being killed by those robots. And last, but certainly not least, Talon tried to kill me with the robots first. The lizard and I aren't exactly on the same side anymore."

Super Penguin responded, "Talon tried to kill you? But why?"

"Well, actually, I have you two to thank for that. When we didn't deliver you the first time, I became expendable and one of their test subjects. I got shocked unconscious, but, luckily, those clunky metal heads thought I was a goner. I've been sneaking around the complex for the last couple days."

The others in the car didn't know how to respond. Super Penguin broke the silence awkwardly. "Well...welcome to the team, I guess." He chuckled and gave the hyena a half-hearted pat on the back.

"Thanks," Henry replied. "So, what's the plan?"

"Simple," Super Penguin responded confidently. "Break a bunch of robots and knock out a big, ugly lizard!"

"Sounds like fun," Annie added, "but we need to have more than that figured out. There are going to be people down there who need help too."

"Alright," Super Penguin conceded. "Sam, you stay with the van. Help get as many people as you can away from downtown. Then, we need to find a way to stop all the robots. Any ideas there, Cackle?"

"I remember hearing Talon talk to the guy who made these things," Henry answered. "Someone nearby is giving them orders, but it's got pretty good range. Our best bet is probably going to be destroying them manually."

"Alright!" Super Penguin wrapped up the impromptu meeting. "So back to the original plan. Evacuate downtown, break a bunch of robots, and then, if the big, ugly lizard shows up.... we knock him out."

Sam continued to speed toward the scene. Talon made it easy to find: follow the smoke floating into the skyline and the sounds of destruction. The van arrived and came to an abrupt halt.

"Oh my gosh." Annie gasped as the rest of the crew watched in a stupor. Complete chaos had broken out in downtown Eagle City. Smoke, fire, lasers blasting. People everywhere running scared. To the left of the van, a young mother sheep hid in an alleyway protecting her lamb. To the van's right, two goats stood on either side of a third, helping him limp to safety.

"Sam's going to need help getting people out," Super Penguin called. "Annie, you're the strongest of all of us. We can use that fighting these robots, but these guys need it more. Stay with Sam and usher people away. Henry and I will start taking out the bots."

The rest of the team nodded in affirmation.

Super Penguin opened the van's side door. "Alright, LET'S GO!"

***

The town was in chaos. Screams could be heard nearby and in the distance. An overwhelming array of madness was visible in every direction. Super Penguin did a quick inventory of his supplies. He didn't have much; besides the cape, he had his stun baton collapsed in his right pocket and two smoke bombs in his left. His new partner Henry watched. "Man, I should have hung onto that gun." The hyena walked over to a steel trashcan. He removed the lid and looked it over. "Eh," he shrugged his shoulders, "this should do. Okay, so where do we start?" The two gazed across the landscape. There was trouble in every direction. Seemingly on cue, a loud explosion came from Town Square, the heart of downtown. Without saying a word, the two sprinted in that direction.

As they ran, they crossed into a cloud of smoke. The penguin and hyena could hardly see a foot in front of their faces, but as they pressed on, the smoke grew thinner.

When they reached the square, a swarm of at least twenty robots marched forward, chasing a crowd of citizens. Super Penguin and Henry ran toward the swarm. In stride, Super Penguin launched both of his smoke bombs, one between the robots and the citizens to buy some time for their getaway. The other bomb was tossed between the heroes and their target to catch the bots off guard.

Surrounded by smoke, the bots halted. With no visible target, they had no place to move. Suddenly, through the smoke emerged the two heroes airborne and striking—Super Penguin wielding his electric baton and Henry with his trashcan lid shield. Both struck a bot in the front line and knocked them to the ground. Super Penguin shocked the bot in the head. Sparks flew, and the robot twitched uncontrollably before collapsing into a heap.

Meanwhile, Henry Cackle fought with brute force using the steel lid to bash his bot with a strong blow to the head. The strike was strong enough to destroy the bot instantly, but also crumbled the lid on that side; now the lid was nearly half its original size. "Crud!" Henry said as he looked down at the damaged weapon.

In the corner of his eye, Henry saw the red light he had seen at DragonCorp—the half-a-second warning before the deadly laser beam was emitted from the robot's arm. In a flash, the laser shot out, and, as a reflex, the hyena blocked the beam with the crumbled lid. What he didn't expect was for the beam to ricochet off the steel. It careened right back to its source. *BANG!* The robot's head exploded and knocked out the rest of the crowd of bots.

The penguin and hyena locked eyes, and their faces shared a look of shock that morphed into a smirk.

A few blocks away, Annie and Sam continued their evacuation efforts. Annie would go into a building, bring out everyone that would follow, and take them to Sam's van. Sam would then transport the group outside of the danger zone, and, by the time he returned, Annie had the next building cleared.

Sam parked the van and waited for the next group. Annie took two steps out of the building when she spotted Lyla. The tigress was on the rooftop across the street. She held a rocket launcher on her shoulder and was aiming it at Sam's van. "SAM! GET OUT!" Annie screamed and pointed at the rooftop. Sam looked at his friend through the passenger window and then to where she was pointing.

Annie watched her friend open the door and get out and then watched the rocket shoot toward the van. Members of her group screamed when the missile exploded. The screams caught Layla's attention, and from a distance, she locked eyes with Annie. She was torn with an impossible decision: leave her friend and save the citizens or risk the group's safety to find Sam.

"Look! Those robots are coming this way!" a rabbit in the group screamed. "Where do we go?"

Annie left her friend for the group. "This way! Be quick, and keep your heads down," the polar bear directed as she led the group away on foot.

***

Lyla had taken the stairs and reached the ground floor. She looked out into the destruction and pulled out her walkie-talkie. "Sir, there's a resistance here. I saw that bear we've had a few run-ins with, and Sam Hart was here. The rumors were true."

Talon answered, "I knew that goody-two-shoes Hart was still out there. I assume that if you saw him you...."

"Yes, sir. Launched a rocket right at him. There's no way he survived the blast."

"You said that last time."

"I don't make the same mistake twice, sir."

"Very good. We've spotted the penguin two blocks north and two blocks west. It appears he is with your friend Henry Cackle, also back from the dead...finish them off too please.

"On it." She clipped the walkie-talkie back onto her hip and set to move toward her next two targets. She took a couple of steps, but then a seed of doubt snuck into Lyla's mind. "Ugh," she said to herself and went to make sure she had finished off the lion before she started her next objective. Lyla walked toward the smoldering van.

Not much of the van remained—its smoldering frame and a few parts scattered around it. Pieces had flown in every direction. The tigress scanned the area, frustrated, but she saw no evidence at first. A few feet to her right, Lyla saw Sam's cane. She bent over, picked it up and...

WAM!

A large rock crashed into the back of her head. The blow brought Lyla to her knees, and she had just enough time to look behind her and see her assailant. There stood Sam. His already messy mane now had charred tips, and most of his body was dripping wet. Sam picked up his cane, cocked a sadistic smile, and mockingly waved goodnight to Lyla has she collapsed face-first onto the asphalt.

"You're alive?" Sam heard Annie's voice behind him.

"Thanks to you," he cracked a smile. "Your warning gave me just enough time to jump into the sewers..." Annie stopped listening and interrupted the lion's explanation with a great, big bear hug that lifted Sam off the ground. He chuckled as he was set back down. "I'm glad you're okay too, kid, but we still got work to do." Sam pulled a pair of handcuffs out of his pocket. Lyla's motionless arms were held behind her back and wrapped around the light post. "We'll come get her when we're all done...maybe."

***

A few blocks away, Super Penguin and Henry continued to fight the robot army. "That's twenty-two for me. How many have you got?" hollered Henry.

Super Penguin shook his head and smirked as he used his staff to take down the last two nearby bots. "I didn't know we were counting, but I'll say I got at least twenty-three. Do you think this is the last of them?"

Henry didn't answer. Instead, his attention was a hundred yards behind Super Penguin. "We're probably done with the bots, but this doesn't look good." Super Penguin turned around and saw a slick, silver tank driving down the middle of the road. "Whaddya think the odds are it's a DragonCorp tank?"

"I'd say there's a pretty good chance, Henry."

The tank drove closer and closer. Meanwhile, the penguin and the hyena stood their ground, waiting for the first sign of an attack. But no attack was made. The tank got within twenty feet from them and stopped. The hatch lifted, and the Komodo dragon General Talon emerged. The general stared at the two heroes with a menacing grin. "Well, well, well, if it isn't the world-famous Super Penguin. And this must be your new sidekick. Does he have a name yet? Maybe 'The Traitor,' he couldn't beat the penguin, so he joined him? Oh, how about Captain Failure! He couldn't do anything right the first time, even dying—"

"That's enough, Talon," Super Penguin cut him off. "Your plan stops now!" He and Henry stood ready to brawl, fists clenched with their eyes focused on the lizard.

Talon stared at Super Penguin. "You're a brave little bird... stupid...but brave." General Talon pulled himself out of the hatch and quickly leapt off the tank. When he landed in the middle of the road, the ground seemingly shook. The lizard stood up from his crouched landing pose and brushed the dust off his suit. He stepped toward the sidewalk and offered one final bargain. "I'll give you each one final chance to stand down. Join me...or die."

Neither Super Penguin nor Henry answered.

The lizard turned his back to his foes and continued walking toward the sidewalk. "I'll take that as a NO!" Talon yelled. He showed off his brute strength by ripping a light post out of the ground. Talon held it with both hands above his head and threw it directly at Super Penguin and Henry.

The hyena hopped over, and the penguin plunged under. The post slammed into the wall behind them, loosening the bricks from the mortar. After missing with the throw, Talon charged his opponents. He aimed for Super Penguin first; with teeth snarling and claws at the ready, he lunged at the bird. Super Penguin stuck his staff into the ground and vaulted over Talon. In a second effort, the general swung his tail and knocked the bird into a nearby car. No sooner than the penguin crashed into the vehicle, he stood to his feet and Talon was lunging at him again. This time, Henry dove at Talon, knocking him off course. Talon was momentarily on his back with the hyena pinning him down. Henry got in two claw swipes to Talon's face before he was shoved off and thrown into the same car. Both heroes got to their feet quickly but were again unprepared for a charging General Talon. Super Penguin to the left and Henry to the right, they both dove out of the way, causing the lizard to run head first into the vehicle.

The car bent in half and skidded across the pavement. Talon let out a ferocious "ROAR!" He gripped the smashed car door with both sets of claws, dug in, and ripped the door off the hinges. Another "ROAR!" and Talon chucked the door at Super Penguin.

The hero ducked and rolled underneath the projectile. The door crashed into the wall behind him.

A trashcan lid, flung like a frisbee, struck Talon in the head. He turned and faced its thrower, Henry. Talon quickly stepped towards him, claws out, ready to tear into the hyena.

BZZZZZZTTTTTT

Super Penguin leapt onto Talon's back and electrified him with the staff. Talon fell to his knees then on all fours. Super Penguin kept the current of electricity flowing, and Talon was neutralized. "I'll hold him here. Go get help, Henry." The hyena looked on hesitantly. Sirens blared nearby. "GO! I got this!"

Henry ran toward the sound.

Super Penguin held the general down with his electrified staff, but then there was a short skip. Then another. Batteries were running low. Super Penguin pressed on, but with each skip, Talon adjusted himself to retaliate. Battery dead.

Super Penguin stepped back. He reset his staff, trying to get more out of it but failed.

Off.

On.

Small spark.

Off.

On.

Smaller spark.

Each time, the spark was weaker, and it disappeared sooner than the try before.

Talon rose to his feet. With his back to Super Penguin he let out his loudest "ROAR!"

He turned around, faced the penguin and marched towards him, each step a little bit faster than the one before.

Super Penguin stood his ground. When Talon drew close, he swung the staff over his head, leapt in the air to strike and...

UGH!

Talon snatched Super Penguin with one hand right out of the air. "You're done, bird." The reptile squeezed the air out of the penguin, until he began to turn blue. "No, not satisfying enough." Talon thought aloud. He lightened his grip, just enough for the bird to breathe. Super Penguin got one gasp of air before...

SLAM!

General Talon grabbed Super Penguin by the throat, lifted the penguin above his head, and slammed him into the ground. With his hand still around his throat and Super Penguin now in a small crater in the asphalt, Talon snarled his menacing snarl. "This is where the road ends for you, bird. You insignificant, unimportant waste of space and time. Did you really think a weakling like you could beat me? Any last words, bird?"

"It's...not over...yet Talon."

The general laughed. "Oh really? Then let's end it now!"

A whistling noise preceded a *THUD!* as the chunk of asphalt smashed into the back of Talon's head. The lizard turned around with a scowl that morphed into a menacing smile as he saw Sam. "I had a feeling the tiger's news was too good to be true, but it looks I'll have to finish you off myself. Today's my lucky day. Once I'm done with you, I'll go back and finish off the bird." Talon released his grip, rose to his feet with his eyes were on the lion. The lizard smiled menacingly as wide as his mouth could go.

Sam crouched readily with his left side slightly closed to his opponent. He extended his left arm, opened up his paw, and brushed his fingers back toward himself. "Bring it, punk," said the lion.

Talon pounced toward Sam. While the lizard was airborne, Sam somersaulted out of the way and limped back up to his feet.

The general pounced again. Sam tried to avoid the attack a second time but was caught by Talon's claws. The lizard tackled the lion to the ground. They rolled over each other, but Talon ended up on top. His back now to Super Penguin, Talon gripped Sam's neck. "Did you really think you were a match for me, old man?" the lizard hissed.

Sam fought to catch his breath through his exhaustion and Talon's grip.

"I knew I couldn't beat you," he paused to catch his breath again, "but I knew with a little distraction, he could. Rule Number One." Sam smiled as he collapsed.

Talon turned, with his claws still clinging to Sam's neck. Super Penguin was gone. The lizard's head darted left, then right, then left again. Where did the penguin go?

THWACK!

Super Penguin's staff struck Talon square in the back of his head. Talon released Sam, stumbled forward, and turned around to face his foe.

Now, filled with rage and gripping his staff, Super Penguin shouted, "I used to believe you, Talon. I used to think I was weak and unimportant. I used to think that bigger, stronger guys like you always win no matter the situation. But today, *you're going down!*"

"Awfully big words from such a small bird."

Super Penguin ran toward Talon, screaming his battle cry. "AHHHHHHHHH!"

Suddenly, something remarkable happened that not even the penguin himself could explain. The hero began to glow with a light purple hue. As the penguin ran faster and closer to Talon, the purple light grew stronger and brighter.

Steps away from his foe, Super Penguin started emitting purple sparks from his body that then carried into his staff. Super Penguin stuck his staff into the ground, propelling himself into the air. Now, he was just a few feet from the lizard.

The hero somersaulted mid-air, pulled the staff over his head, and swung down toward Talon's head. As he did, the mysterious energy left the penguin and transferred itself into the staff with a ball of energy at the tip.

VOOOOOOOSH!

At contact, the energy ball was released. It blasted purple energy and sparks in every direction and sent Talon flailing some twenty yards into a brick wall. The lizard was knocked unconscious.

Super Penguin felt equal parts accomplished, confused, and exhausted. He'd done it. He'd beaten Talon. "What happened to me?" he thought aloud. Super Penguin dropped his staff and stared at his flippers as two more purple sparks shot out of each. The hero looked around for witnesses. Only Sam. Nobody else. He observed Sam for a moment and saw his mentor was still breathing. Relieved but exhausted, Super Penguin collapsed onto the pavement.

***

"Hey, Super Penguin, are you there?" *snap* *snap* *snap*

The hero opened his eyes and found Henry above him.

Behind his friend stood Lieutenant Boone with four police officers. General Talon was a few feet away, handcuffed with his arms behind his back. "There's been a misunderstanding I..."

Super Penguin looked down; he was handcuffed too, but his arms were in the front.

Sirens blared nearby, growing closer and closer. Moments later, Mayor Mooney, a wolf, arrived with a police escort from Police Chief Cooper, a raccoon, and Deputy Chief Yu, a sheep.

"Great work, boys!" Mayor Mooney said as he clapped his paws together. He tugged on his suit jacket and addressed his small audience. "We finally caught the criminal who's been terrorizing our streets, and if it weren't for one of Eagle City's best citizens, it never would have happened. Great work, General Talon. Chief Cooper, I'll let you handle the penguin, but don't take him away until the media gets here. This will be a great photo op." He licked his paws and slicked back his hair. "Chief Cooper, why is the general in handcuffs? Let him go, at once!"

Two of the officers walked behind Talon to obey the Mayor's request.

"Hold it! Keep those cuffs on!" shouted Boone.

"Excuse me?" the General questioned.

"Boone, stand down," Chief Cooper directed but was ignored.

Annie appeared behind the police officers with her reporter gear and press badge around her neck.

Mooney saw her. "Oh, perfect! The press is here!" He slicked back his hair again. "Let's get a photo of the penguin being put into the back of the car with handcuffs on and—"

"Lieutenant Boone," Super Penguin interrupted, "can we trust Deputy Yu?"

"What?" Mooney shrieked. "Keep quiet, penguin!"

Boone nodded at Super Penguin.

"Deputy Yu, I have evidence of crimes committed and conspired to commit by General Talon. There's a tape recorder in my pocket. May I reach for it?

Yu moved toward the penguin. "Yes." She looked at Boone. "I hope you know what you're doing!" Boone nodded.

Super Penguin removed his tape recorder, turned the volume to the max, and hit play.

"... I'd like to share with you my master plan. You've been a worthwhile adversary despite being a royal pain in my tail, and before you die, I want you to know exactly how we will eventually beat you, no, destroy you and your precious city..."

"That's enough," Yu instructed. She looked at two of Boone's officers. "We'll finish this investigation back at the station, but I've heard enough to make an arrest; get him in the car." The officers obeyed, and Yu turned back around to the penguin.

"There's more, ma'am," Super Penguin added. He selected another file on his recorder.

"I'm sure you already know, little bird, but in case you didn't, DragonCorp owns this city! The mayor, the chief of police, and most of the force. Anyone with any real power in this city reports to ME!"

Mooney and Cooper's eyes doubled in size. They both turned around to run and were surprised to find their former chief, Sam Hart, standing behind them. He smiled, shook his head, and twirled his finger to tell them to turn back around. When they did, Yu stood with a disapproving smirk. She then looked up to Sam.

"Good to see you again, Chief Hart," Yu said with a smile as she cuffed the raccoon and wolf.

"Good to be seen again." He chuckled.

Deputy Chief Yu led the crooks into the squad car, shut the door, and tapped the roof. "Good to go, Rick."

She turned back. "So, Mr. Super Peng—" but he had disappeared. She turned to where Sam stood. He was gone too. Yu turned to Annie, who *was* still there. "Where did they go?"

Annie shrugged with a smile.

"Would you tell me if you knew?"

The bear shrugged again, still smiling.

"Okay, well if you see them again, tell them I say, 'Thank you, and job well done.'"

"*If* I see them, I'll let them know."

***

One week later

Annie sat at her newsroom desk typing up her sixth story related to the DragonCorp crimes.

"Hey Annie!" a familiar voice bellowed.

"Paul!" she exclaimed excitedly, "welcome back!"

"Glad to be back! Although, I don't think Howie was too excited to give me my desk or my beat back."

Annie laughed. "How was your meeting with Trunk?"

"It wasn't too bad. Apparently, being half right was good enough for his dad. I had to agree not to accuse any more players of crimes until *after* Super Penguin catches them."

She laughed. "That's probably a pretty good rule to follow! Hey, are you good for Tina's for lunch? I've missed our lunch-time meetings."

"Absolutely! Let me go get situated, and then I'll come back with my schedule for the day and we can figure out a time."

Paul left Annie's desk and went back to the sports area. A small note, folded several times, had been left in the center of his desk.

I know where your power comes from. If you are interested, meet me where it happened tonight at midnight.

Paul scanned the room looking for a sign as to where this note had come from. Everyone in the newsroom seemed to be working and paying no attention to the penguin. Just then Annie approached. "Hey, sorry, um....you're going to want to see this." She led Paul to the break room where a crowd had begun to form around the TV.

"...*another interesting chapter unfolded today in the Dragon-Corp investigation. As previously reported, DragonCorp's General Tobias Talon built several robots designed to take over the city. Well, today, newly appointed Police Chief Martha Yu announced that those robots have gone missing....*"

Annie and Paul locked eyes and nodded simultaneously.

Paul went back into the sports department and found his colleague. "Hey, Howie, I had something come up. Can you cover for me tonight?"

"QUACK!" The duck's excitement overpowered him. "You know it's a playoff game, right?"

"Yeah, something pretty big happened....so ugh.... thanks!"

Paul left the office, got into his car, and headed toward his next adventure.

TO BE CONTINUED...